Sea Wraith

The Meranda Haley Series
Book 2

JJ Lynn Daniels

B. SHEPHERD
PUBLICATIONS
Books that Inspire Antifragility

Contents

Also by JJ Lynn Daniels

The Meranda Haley Series

Ghosts of the Bayou

Sea Wraith

The Metal's Bane Series

Verdigris

Tarnish

Rust

For John
Your support means everything

SEA WRAITH

THE MERANDA HALEY SERIES: BOOK TWO

JJ LYNN DANIELS

Chapter One

I cursed my feet for not being faster. I cursed the creature before me for stepping in my way and bringing me up short. I cursed the man I was chasing as he took a left at the end of the alleyway and disappeared. The concrete of the buildings on either side of the alley echoed the sounds of his boot falls back to me. Mocking me.

An angry squeak sounded from the creature in front of me, drawing my attention back to it. Though I had hardly taken my eyes off it since it appeared. You couldn't turn your back on a beast like that. Its white fluffy hide was a defense, an innocent suit it wore. No one would suspect that under those long floppy ears was the mind of a killer.

I should have jumped over it. The second it appeared, I should have told my feet to jump and been on my way, but instead I drew up short. I'd lost my nerve. Master Harnock would certainly have something to say about that if he ever found out about it.

The kell bared its teeth. Or maybe it always looked like that. I hadn't gotten close enough to one before to know if that sharp canine on the left always stuck out that way.

"He won't hurt you," a voice said. A stranger stepped out of the same doorway the kell had emerged from seconds before. It was the kind of doorway you wouldn't even notice if you had been walking down this alley in the middle of the day. Just one more door in an alley that half this city used to cut across streets without running into traffic.

"Says you," I said, careful not to make any sudden movements lest the kell take it as a threat.

"They're not dangerous," the stranger said. "That's a misunderstanding."

Congestion built up in my nose. Just being this close to that fur made my eyes water.

"I guess that depends on your definition of dangerous."

The man's mouth curled into a sneer. He wore a worker's jumpsuit, white, paint splattered. I stepped back as he leaned forward and scooped up the kell. He murmured soft words into the white hide and glared at me between the ears. I could swear the kell winked at me. With one last snort in my direction, the man returned through the doorway in the side of the alley and slammed it, taking the kell with him.

"Scared of bunnies now, are we?"

I tensed at Samuel's voice behind me. How much had he seen?

"It's not a bunny; it's a kell," I said, allowing an ounce of annoyance into my voice. Maybe that would take some of the burning from my cheeks.

Samuel's chuckle was a low rumble behind me. I huffed out a breath.

"Kell aren't real," he said.

"You sound awfully sure of that," I snapped, finally spinning around to face him. "Next time, you can take your chances with a creature that can strip flesh from your bones in ten seconds flat."

The lighting in the alley was dim, but I could tell he was holding back laughter. His shoulders shook from the effort.

"Did you get Paulo?"

Samuel held his arms out from his side emphasizing their emptiness.

I groaned.

"He had a buddy in a car waiting for him. We didn't stand a chance even if your way hadn't been barred by a— fluffy bunny." His smile flashed white in the darkness. Too bright in his dark face, dark clothes. Damn his humor and his dental hygiene.

I let out a grumble and made to stalk past him, but immediately stepped my left boot into a puddle. *Just great.* This night was going from bad to worse at an alarming pace. I shook my leg and tried not to look at Samuel.

"Let's head back to the Agency and regroup," Samuel said. His voice wasn't teasing anymore. It was as though he knew how close I was to throwing a fit right here in this dark New Orleans alleyway no matter how unbecoming it might be. "There's gotta be something more we're missing."

We drove back to the Agency in silence. My mind took advantage of the quiet to throw back at me every mistake we'd made in this investigation. It was a longer list than I'd liked—starting with taking the case in the first place.

Today alone had been a master class in screw ups.

I had spent the afternoon finding Paulo's safe house. A combination of wild guesswork and asking pointed questions to the right people got us the address.

No one was supposed to be there at this time of night. At least that's what I had been led to believe. I should have pushed harder, dug deeper. I might have known it was a waste of time.

When I picked the lock to the safe house and pushed the door open, it was easy to see there was nothing worth finding in that rundown apartment. A couple of two-bit thieves who were content to ply their craft on citizens of this city who were only marginally better off than they. These were not master minds. Not the type to steal what we were looking for.

We shouldn't have even bothered chasing them, but Paulo giving me a shove as he raced for the door pissed me off. I didn't even have to check behind me. I knew Samuel was right on my heels when I pursued them into the humid Louisiana darkness.

It would have been nice to catch them. Even if they weren't the thieves we were looking for, maybe they could give us another lead. Instead of a lead, I was left with a soaked boot dripping into the passenger side floorboards of Dad's car.

The bright lights of New Orleans passed outside the car window. Flashes of neon advertising palm readings and tarot cards. In the light of day, most questionable establishments stayed quiet, but this late at night they were free to advertise to those passing by. Absentmindedly, I wondered if I should ask one of them for a lead. Probably not. Most of these psychics were worthless, I knew. If you have to advertise that hard to get customers, your abilities were more than likely crap.

Nothing like my aunt.

We somehow made it back to the Agency without Samuel cracking another joke about white, fluff-clad killers. The dark wooden sign announcing my father's business of the last two decades creaked in the slight breeze that blew up the street. Sugar maple leaves danced around our feet, swirling in shades of red and orange. My boot would have crunched on one if it hadn't been so busy squelching at me.

I pushed open the front door and the bell above it jingled happily, greeting us. It was an odd sound in the middle of the night. Out of place in the dark hallway that split the Agency in half between my father's office and Madame LaMontagne's parlor.

Samuel's grandmother, my aunt, was home for the night. One of the few things to go right this evening. I knew she'd ask about the case. I wasn't keen on reporting how poorly our one shot at pulling this Agency out of debt was going.

I automatically flipped on the light in Dad's office as I entered. The small room greeted me with a familiarity that made me want to relax, but I was too wound up from the chase to give in. Samuel seemed to have no trouble relaxing, promptly falling onto the old green couch that sat against the wall beside the door and stretching out like a cat. Half of his legs stuck off the end of the couch, but that didn't seem to bother him in the slightest.

I ripped off my black combat boots and set them beside the low bookshelf that held Dad's old beat-up detective novels. I laid my soaked sock over the boot toes, hoping the elevation would help it dry quicker. My hands shook as I stood again.

Dad's desk was stocked with everything I could need; I'd made sure of it. I yanked open the top drawer. There, in all its cellophane glory, atop a stack of overdue bills was the one thing on my mind. I ripped open the package and shoved three pretzels into my mouth before turning to face Samuel again.

"What are we missing?"

Samuel's sigh came from somewhere deep inside of him, whooshing out like a tidal wave. "I don't know. Everything?"

"That's not helpful," I said.

"What do you want me to say, Mer?" Samuel asked. His bicep flexed under his black sweatshirt as he crossed his arms over his chest. "We took a case from an employer we've never worked with before, who refuses to tell us anything about his business, or even *what* of his was stolen. We've been chasing dead end leads for over a week now. Paulo and his gang were the last on my list of potential suspects, and even that was a hunch of a hunch. I'm tapped out."

"Well, tap back in," I said. I knew it wasn't fair, but my cheeks burned at the words he was saying. Even if they were all true. "Mr. Poincare has offered us more than enough to pull this Agency out of the red. It's one case. We find his stolen goods and bam, we're back. We might even be able to pay some bills and get Internet back in this place. Do you have any idea how annoying it is to have to sneak in searches at the *Academy*?"

"None of that matters if we can't find the damn thing," Samuel said.

"It's a test," I said, shaking the remainder of the pretzel pack into my mouth. "He said he wants to be sure we're good enough to earn the payout. We don't only have to find what was stolen; we have to figure out what it is first. That's the deal."

"Well, it's a dumb deal," Samuel said.

I shrugged. "Do you see any other clients breaking down our door?"

My phone buzzed and I pulled it out of my back pocket. *What now? A client would be nice. Nope. Dammit.*

Something must have shown on my face because Samuel bit back whatever retort he was about to unleash on me. "What is it?"

"A parent chaperone canceled for the field trip tomorrow."

"They want you to work," he said.

"I need the money. Maybe it will give me a chance to think about other leads we can pursue."

Samuel made a humming noise.

"Or maybe I should try Oleksandr again. If he could give us more information on what the Poincare Corporation does. Maybe we could get a lead on what was stolen."

Samuel groaned.

"You could call him," I suggested and relished the horrified look my partner-in-stopping-crime gave me.

"No thanks. You want to use the bloodsucker, you call him."

"What do you want to try next?"

Samuel shrugged. "I still have some contacts in the underground that haven't completely abandoned me. Maybe I can try them."

"I'll need the car tomorrow to get to the museum." I grabbed the keys off Dad's desk. "Come on, I'll drive you home."

"You're such a gentleman," Samuel said, his six-foot-frame folding in a mock curtsy.

"Well, a delicate flower like yourself shouldn't be walking the streets of New Orleans alone this late in the evening. Who knows what might happen."

"Ha ha," Samuel said without a hint of amusement. "That's enough of that."

It wasn't—I still held the car door open for him in the parking lot.

The glare was worth it.

Chapter Two

The New Orleans Museum of Natural History stood in a two-story brick building just west of the French Quarter. It had been built in the post-portal world. Originally the building had been a bank, housing financial documents and lock boxes. After the portals opened and the melusines were pushed back into the Gulf, people didn't have much use for banks. The security of keeping your most important belongings in a locked building was trumped by the need to get out of Dodge quickly.

The building would have remained empty if some historically-minded member of the city's elite hadn't decided that we had better start preserving some of New Orleans history. Almost immediately the building was converted into a museum. Now, instead of bored tellers and patrons, the rooms were filled with uniformed students, and families with small children who sought refuge from the humidity outside.

"Ms. Haley, they have a haunted ship exhibit." Linette Stevens tugged on the sleeve of my tan blouse, pulling me forward. A massive poster in the lobby, hanging precariously over the kiosks to buy tickets, shouted the museum's most recent acquisition.

Pulled from the depths and dangers of the Gulf.
A smuggler's ship holding secrets untold.
Sea Wraith awaits!
Tickets $5

"It doesn't say it's *haunted*," an older boy whose name I didn't know sniped at Linette.

"Pulled from the depths," Linette said, gesturing animatedly at the sign. "How much more haunted can you get."

"It's not haunted," the boy insisted. "Isn't that right Ms. Haley?"

Linette's wide blue eyes stared up at me, begging me to prove her right. I couldn't, truthfully. Most ghosts from shipwrecks were guided on to their final resting place or remained in the ocean. There was hardly ever a time when a ship came back to land with some haunting attached to it.

"I'm sure they wouldn't put something in the museum that could hurt you," I told them both. Squinting at the sign again, I had to admit the image behind the text looked like nothing so much as a cursed galleon. "Haunted or not."

Linette's eyes lit up. "I'm going to see a ghost," she whispered.

I bit back the chastisement that rose in my chest. The girl didn't truly understand what she was saying. She'd never seen the harm a real spirit could cause, hurting and lost in this plane beyond its time. I couldn't fault her for being excited. She was nine.

On a normal day of teaching at Crescent City Academy, I handled high schoolers. I had far more experience with them than I did their elementary student counterparts at the school. But money is money, and if I had to chaperone an elementary field trip to make mortgage, I'd do it. I caught sight of my best friend across the room. It wasn't so bad when I could convince Brigitte to tag along.

The gaggle of students moved forward, surging toward a caste skeleton of a werewolf in hybrid form. Brigitte read off the sign in front of the display. It was the typical human propaganda about werewolves being a danger to humans, highlighting the way their claws could rend and tear. Just more fuel to replicate the structure of this society, the separation between the humans and the other creatures who called this city home. I rolled my eyes and looked around the room.

The blue and white tartan uniforms made it easy to track the students under our charge. There were two other teachers helping to manage the chaos, but with twenty children it was still a chore.

A child I couldn't recognize from behind pushed on the bar for an emergency exit. I was too far across the room to catch him, and I cringed automatically at the incoming alarm. None came. An unalarmed fire door? Money must just be that tight for a museum these days. Heaven forbid there's actually a fire. A fellow teacher pulled the student back and squatted down to give him a talking to.

I herded one errant head of pigtails back to the group as we entered the next room. We passed through heavy, scarlet curtains held back by golden cord. This was the main event —the exhibit that garnered all the attention. The museum had pulled out all the stops to make this one worth the five-dollar charge. They even dimmed the lights and placed spotlights on the ship in case you had any trouble remembering why you entered this room.

They hadn't needed to. Oohs and ahs sounded from the group of students before me. The ship was breath-taking. All they had managed to salvage, or possibly all they could fit in this room, was the forecastle and the prow. The mainsail hung in tattered cloth around the foremast. A voice boomed through the overhead speakers:

"Pulled from the depths of the Gulf, the Sea Wraith *would have been magnificent in its day. Perhaps used by pirates to smuggle booty,"* the few snickers from the children at the word were hushed by a stern look, *"perhaps used in service to a king to hunt pirates. Not much is known about the galleon other than its size and beauty. No logs exist in known history to tell of its exploits. But one thing we can know for sure—as the ship went down, so did the captain, his body tied to the ship's wheel in one final act of honor and loyalty. As is tradition. For a captain always goes down with his ship."* The recorded voice ended abruptly, and a small murmuring could be heard among the students. A slight hiss sounded from the speakers and recorded noises took over as of being on board a wooden vessel, all creaking and sails snapping in the wind. The smell of saltwater hit me almost immediately. I closed my eyes and took a deep breath. The scent of home.

I walked around the room, staring along with the children. The name *Sea Wraith* had been painted onto the side of the ship's prow. The paint looked almost too fresh for the vessel to be as old as was claimed. Dark blue letters outlined in silver. I had seen shipwrecks beneath the waves. Those that were decades old didn't have paint this well preserved.

I wondered absentmindedly if the museum had repainted the lettering. That couldn't be right. They wouldn't do that to an artifact of history, would they?

I circled around the prow and finally noticed the figurehead. I hadn't seen her before. She was melusine, a bold choice considering the dangers they posed in the waters of the Gulf, carved into the dark wood with an expert hand. Her tail draped down the starboard side of the prow, intricate scales stained blue-green. Her wooden hair cascaded down her chest, covering her breasts, the long waves trailing to her navel. Her face looked almost morose. The sides of her mouth drooped, and her eyes focused down. When the ship was on the sea, I was sure she would be looking down into the waters before the prow. At the lonely curve of her mouth, I was struck with the overwhelming feeling that she had lost something and couldn't ever get it back.

A wave of ocean scent hit me again, nearly bowling me over. This time, it didn't smell like home. Something was wrong. It smelled like death. My heart pounded in my chest. Sweat broke out on my brow. Something was rotten with this ship. Something deep. I made eye contact with Brigitte and gestured to the curtained entrance. She nodded and I ducked out.

I pressed myself against the wall beside the exhibit entrance and took a few deep breaths. I had to go back in there. I couldn't just abandon my fellow chaperones to the mercy of the fourth graders. But first I needed to breathe. I leaned forward and stared at the shiny floor between my heeled boots. Breathe in, breathe out. I could still smell the stench from the ship.

"You look seasick," a voice sounded to my left. I jerked upright.

It was the blond man from the bar. The man who

smelled of salt and sea and home. He wore the same style loose cotton shirt. The white fabric only made his tanned skin appear darker; his shoulders stand out broader. His blue eyes bore into me just as they had when we'd first met. Just as at Baxter's, his gaze captivated me. Made me want to blush. He was too close; I could feel the heat of him.

I tried to step sideways away from him and was rewarded with a head rush. I leaned back against the wall behind me and willed the room to stop spinning.

"The exhibit can be disorienting," he said, his voice low so only I could hear. "It's the scent they pump into the room to make it more realistic."

"You a museum expert?" I asked, squeezing my eyes shut as my stomach rolled.

He chuckled low, a rumble that made me wonder what it would feel like if my hand was on his chest when he made that noise.

"Here."

He pressed a package into my hand, and I snapped my eyes open at the familiar crinkle.

"Pretzels, really?"

The stranger shrugged. "I find it helps to settle the stomach. Especially when the sea is the cause."

"Well, thank you," I said, unsure what else to say. Most in this city didn't go out of their way to help someone they didn't even know. I pulled open the package and shook a few pretzels into my hand before tossing them into my mouth.

"What are you doing here anyway?"

"Maybe I just like museums," he said. "Maybe I'm a student of the arts."

I raised an eyebrow at him. "Or maybe you're following

me. First Baxter's and now here. A girl might get the wrong idea."

He leaned in close enough that I could see the slight sheen of sweat on his neck. "Don't get your hopes up," he whispered. "You're not *all* I think about."

Goosebumps raised the hairs on my arms. I wanted to fight off the uncomfortable fluttering in my gut with a phrase of biting sarcasm, but my mind was blank. Frankly, a terrible time for my wit to abandon me.

"Goodbye, Meranda." His breath was warm against my cheek. When he pulled back, a coldness chilled me.

He turned and walked back across the lobby and out the front doors of the museum. The only evidence he'd even been there was the pretzel bag in my hand and the flush on my cheeks.

Brigitte stepped up beside me. "Who was that?"

I touched a hand to my face, cooling the redness there. "I have no idea."

Chapter Three

"Put your back into it," Harnock called from across the room. "This should be easy."

I adjusted my grip on the rope, winding it around my right hand and leaning back, using all my weight to move the sledge. The platform atop the structure was loaded down with sandbags. Each sandbag weighed around twenty-five pounds. There were five of them on the top and the rope attached was easily another ten pounds.

"Easy for you to say," I answered through gritted teeth. "Your back is twice the size of mine."

Geoff Harnock, master-at-arms for Crescent City Academy, let out a barking laugh. "It didn't get that way by accident. Come on, pull again."

The Crescent City Academy gymnasium smelled of rubber and sweat and dirty metal bleachers. The students had all gone home for the day. It was only Harnock and me in the echoing gym. Well, us and the sledge.

I gave one last effort on the rope and managed to slide the platform forward nearly a full inch.

"You know what would make this easier," I said. "Wheels."

Geoff crossed his arms. "Yes, but that would defeat the purpose."

"Break?" I asked, dropping the rope.

"You're worse than the students," Geoff growled, but he jerked his head toward the bleachers, and I gratefully flopped down on one and took up my water bottle.

Geoff crouched on the ground before me, his feet flat on the gym floor, his hips sinking below the level of his knees. He rocked back and forth stretching his legs. Too damn flexible by half. Anytime we worked together, I looked as stiff as a wooden board beside him. Everything he taught me was beyond my capabilities. It was really starting to get on my nerves.

My arms ached; they shook as I lifted the bottle to my lips. The sweat from my brow seeped into my eyes. I had barely slept the night before, all thoughts on the ship. The *not haunted* ship. And the stranger who had appeared again. It all added up to a short mood.

"Finish up and grab your gloves," he said, rising. Stretching time was over, apparently.

I nearly groaned. "We just trained striking yesterday."

"Of course we trained yesterday," the master-at-arms said. "And we will train them today, and tomorrow, and any other day you can spare."

I screwed the lid back on the water bottle, twisting it tighter than strictly necessary. I glared up at him, his massive frame nearly blocked out the lights above, casting a shadow on my face. His blue eyes softened.

"You asked me to train you," he said. "You have to trust that I'm doing that."

It took three rounds of sparring before I was mentally

cursing any training method I had agreed to. By the time we stopped a bruise on my left cheekbone was beginning to bloom and my arms were too weak to hold my fists up any longer.

"You're going to have to train harder than that if you want to survive on the streets of this city, Meranda," he said as we took our seats on the bleachers. He far more gracefully than I.

I took a gulp from my water bottle, breathing hard between sips.

"This is not a kind world you live in," he said. "If you don't train, you get dead."

"Don't lecture me," I said. "I know what's out there. I've been on these streets on my own."

"How did that work out for you?" he asked.

I looked away.

"There was a reason you called me three weeks ago," he pressed. "What was it?"

I didn't answer. I didn't have to. I was sure he could see in my eyes the reasons I was there. If not now, he certainly could have the first day we trained together, when I flinched at his touch. My memories consumed by the feeling of hands around my throat, a hood over my head, the stench of gasoline burning my nostrils...

"You need to understand your 'why?'" he said. "Your reason for being here. If you don't keep that in the forefront of your mind, you'll give up."

I bit back an automatic reply. The habit to protest too quick an impulse. I knew he was right. I asked to be here. I was the one who had come to him, requesting that we train together. How could I be upset at his methods now? If he just wasn't so damn good at everything, it would be easier. I mean, he wasn't even winded. Couldn't he struggle a little?

The silence stretched for a long moment before Harnock cleared his throat.

"Not that teaching is necessarily a safer gig," he said. "Did you hear about the last PTA meeting? It almost came to blows."

I shook my head. The Parent Teacher Association was a place Brigitte liked to volunteer. As a substitute teacher, I wasn't required to work with the PTA, and there was no chance in hell I would be *volunteering* to hang out with parents on a weeknight. Blows, though? For that kind of drama, maybe I'd give it a chance.

"Some of the parents are questioning why their magical children aren't allowed to attend the Academy," he said.

I leaned forward. "What do you mean magical children?"

"You know, the ones who can use magic. Healers, and half-fae, and were-things, and whatnot."

My neck prickled at the thought. Could there actually be change on the horizon? Were the days of elitism at this school coming toward a head?

Harnock started packing his duffel bag. He folded his gloves slowly, the most tenderness I'd seen him show.

He was getting ready to go. I asked the question before he could stand. "What do you think about that?"

Harnock rubbed a hand down his face and blinked a few times. He complained of his contacts often; they must be bothering him again. After a pause, he spoke. "I think if my daughter had a habit of turning into a beast that struck fear into the hearts of men, I'd want her to have the opportunity to be just as educated as the wealthiest in this city. And if the leaders of this city had any sense, they'd want that too."

"Why Master Harnock," I said. "You almost sound like a reformer."

"I've never been one given to groups, Meranda," Harnock growled. "Don't lump me in with one now."

"For what it's worth," I began, "I think having some students here from the marginalized in this city, would be a great benefit to us all." I paused. "Do you think people will start taking sides?"

Harnock rose and slung the duffel bag over his shoulder. "I think people are going to begin seriously considering where they want to stand when this all shakes out."

He turned to go. "I'll see you tomorrow, Meranda."

I watched his back as he walked across the gymnasium. His broad shoulders held proud, his steps sure. Whatever happened, I was sure anyone who valued their life would want to be on his side. I knew I did.

I walked from the Academy grounds, my backpack slung over my shoulder. I could have hitched a ride on a streetcar, but I wanted to walk. My legs were stiff; the walking would stretch them out. The October evening was just beginning. A slight breeze cooled the sweat on my arms and neck, almost leaving behind a chill. The sidewalk was crowded with people and creatures from all walks of life. The sound of a trombone and a clarinet keeping time together lilted on the air. A drum joined them, beating out the rhythm as the players shared the song that moments before only they knew the tune of. I sniffed deep the scent of roasting chicken from a food cart. Damn, I loved October in this city.

I stepped away from the edge of the street as a group of young people in white bedsheets made their way past. Dark holes were cut from the sheets so they could see, and a cacophony of boos and hisses were delivered to anyone who got too close. The city that was filled with monsters somehow still loved its Halloween preparations. A brown-haired shifter, his eyes flashing gold in the light of the setting sun, ducked past me. He carried a plastic skeleton and murmured an apology as his load bumped my shoulder with a rattle. A blue-skinned fae before me barked a curse as the boxes she was carrying fell to the sidewalk. I stopped to help her pick them up.

As I set the last box onto the stack in her arms, a rush of cold hit the back of my neck. I straightened slowly, bringing up my shields just as Florentina had taught me to in the last few weeks. I swiveled my head to see what caused the sensation and caught sight of it almost immediately. A young man, maybe early twenties, the edges of his being flickering on and off this plane. A seeping wound from the side of his forehead dripped blood down into his left eye. His jaw was slack, hanging off one side of his face as though it had been broken by whatever had caused the laceration on his skull. I wanted to go to him. Even with the shields up, I could still feel his pain. His need.

The spirit wandered across the street from one sidewalk to the other, moving away from me. A streetcar passed right through him, he didn't even flinch. He couldn't sense me once my shields were up. The spark that drew him to me, snuffed out so quickly, he must be disoriented. I watched as long as I could until he was swallowed up by the crowd on the other side of the street. My heart ached as I watched him go. I had to find a way to help them cross. Shutting out the static was fine protection, but I couldn't keep ignoring the tug to help them. It was a guilt that rested heavy in my gut.

I turned up the familiar sidewalk that led to Brigitte's house and left behind the bustle of the main street. A cold snap earlier in the season than normal caused the trees that lined the sidewalk to begin showing their red and gold hues. I breathed in the scent of the changing leaves and pulled my backpack higher on my shoulders like a kid excited for his first day of school. Brigitte had demanded I come to dinner at her house after work.

Demand is a strong word. She had suggested that since she was cooking *anyway* it might be nice if I had a 'home cooked meal for once'. The insinuation that I couldn't cook for myself was insulting, but to be fair, I hadn't eaten anything that could be called home cooked in nearly a month. Cereal doesn't count, she assured me. Frankly that seemed unnecessarily limiting, but fine. When your best friend is a healer, and she says you should come to dinner, you say yes.

Besides, with the fall colors coming in, Brigitte was sure to have something warm and comforting on the stove.

I drew up short on the cement walkway leading to her front door. Black smoke billowed out of the front window. Haven't seen that before. I nearly jumped as the front door slammed open and a figure stood in the doorway waving a pink-frilled apron. The frantic apron waving herded the black cloud into the front yard. I nearly laughed when the smoke cleared, and I could finally see who stood in the door-way. Much too tall to be Brigitte.

"Uh, hi," I said.

Samuel coughed twice and threw an arm over his mouth and nose. His tan t-shirt was wrinkled where the apron must have been tied moments before. I tried to picture him with the pink-frills fastened around his waist.

The mental image wouldn't do; I'd need a picture. Maybe Brigitte snapped one before the smoking started.

"Is the rest of the house still standing?" I asked.

"The house is fine," Brigitte's voice preceded her, and she swept onto the porch. She carried a smoking pan before her and threw it onto the grass of the yard. "Someone doesn't know how to tend to a sauté pan."

At my glance, Samuel shrugged. Tears left dark streaks on his cheeks as he coughed again. Brigitte hopped off the porch and started the hose, dousing the pan and turning the black smoke to white steam with a hiss. She wore light blue overalls, the legs rolled up to just below her knee. A cream-colored t-shirt that accentuated her light brown skin showed beneath the overall straps. Her hair was bound up in light blue wrap today, a loosely held-together bun sticking out the top.

"So—" I hesitated. "Dinner is off?"

"Get inside," Brigitte said. "It's only the okra that we lost."

I sat across from Samuel at the round table just outside of the kitchen. Brigitte had insisted we couldn't help her with anything, but I still set the plates and silverware on the table when she wasn't looking. It was the least I could do to make up for whatever horrors Sammy had inflicted on her kitchen. Brigitte had set the nice tablecloth out before I arrived. A woven tan and navy-blue number that matched almost any season. A ceramic cornucopia rested in the center of the round table.

Most of this city liked to skip to Halloween as soon as the weather showed a hint of summer's end. Brigitte would have been happy to forego the entire season to reach Thanksgiving. Not a trace of Halloween could be seen in this house. I had tried to buy her a tiny string of ghosts to hang up on her porch one year and found them across one of the neighbor's garage doors the next day. I didn't try again. I suppose having me for a best friend was ghostly punishment enough.

"What are we celebrating?" Samuel asked, his voice hushed so Brigitte couldn't hear from the kitchen where the sounds of pots and pans crashing together told us that dinner was going swimmingly.

"I didn't know we were celebrating anything," I said. "I'm just here for dinner."

"You guys do that?" Samuel asked. "No special occasion? Just a fancy meal together?"

I nearly laughed. "It's just dinner, Sammy. Nothing fancy about it. If you want to really see a fancy meal, come for Thanksgiving. Brigitte goes all out."

"Almost done," Brigitte called from the kitchen. I winced as a dish hit the floor.

"Did Florentina not cook dinners for you growing up?" I asked.

"Well, sure," Samuel said. He ran a cloth napkin between his fingers. I watched the muscles and tendons in his arms move across each other at the motion. "But not like this."

I tore my eyes away from his arm before he could catch me staring.

"After Mom died, grand-mere didn't do much of anything for a while," Samuel said. "I was too young to remember, but I guess mom was an amazing cook. Grand-mere didn't try."

Samuel looked up and gave me a half smile. "Lots of paper napkins and takeout. Kid-me thought that was just fine, especially if it was pizza."

I reached across the table and touched his hand. "We'll

just have to have you back for Thanksgiving, then. Show you what it's all about. Florentina, too."

Brigitte walked in from the kitchen, and I took my arm back. "Are you inviting people to my house again, Meranda."

I gave her my best shocked face. Mouth open and everything. "Me? No. I would never."

Brigitte placed a covered serving bowl on the table between us and bustled back into the kitchen. "Last time you invited Oleksandr it took me weeks to get the stains out of my rug." Her voice rang out through the kitchen door.

"If the vamp is coming, count me out," Samuel said.

"What? No. You're coming," I said. I called into the kitchen. "It was one spilled drink. Geez, do you forget anything?"

She appeared again, this time with a serving platter. "I most certainly do not. Especially not when it involves my favorite rug."

"You never liked white rugs anyway," I said. I moved the water glasses out of the way so Brigitte could set down the platter. Roasted chicken leg quarters, perfectly crisped. I breathed in the steam. The scent of rosemary and thyme permeated the air.

Brigitte stripped the heat resistant mittens from her hands and untied her apron. "Anything would be better than that garish red he sent to replace it."

"At least he tried," I said.

"Shoot, I almost forgot the broccoli." Brigitte sprang up again and ran to the kitchen.

Samuel snuck a peek beneath the lid of the covered dish. "Red beans and rice."

"Classic," I said.

"That, grand-mere has made."

Brigitte reappeared with what was hopefully the last serving dish. The table was running out of room and my stomach had taken up an ungodly level of growling.

Finally, Brigitte sat down. I scooted my chair in, the squeak of the chair legs on the wooden floorboards as familiar to me as anything.

"Let's say grace," Brigitte said. A calmness came over her, one with which I was intimately acquainted. I wasn't one to pray, but it was her house, and this was her table. I bowed my head.

After a few murmured words of thanks, Brigitte clapped her hands once. "Let's eat."

It was perfect. It always was with Brigitte. The roasted chicken was juicy and tender. The broccoli, a quick replacement for okra, was perfectly steamed. And the red beans and rice? Perfection.

Samuel and I gave all the appropriate words of gratitude to our chef. I tacked on a, 'despite Sammy's best efforts' for good measure and earned a small smile.

"Did you hear about the PTA?" Brigitte asked after dinner, as Samuel took the dishes into the kitchen.

"You're the second person to ask me that today," I told her.

"Well, what do you think?" Brigitte balled up her napkin and looked at me expectantly. Her eyes nearly sparkled in the last rays of light coming in the west-facing front window.

I raised my glass of water to my lips and took a moment before answering. "I think this is a sign of something good coming down the road. But I don't think for one second that change is going to come easily."

"But it will change," Brigitte insisted. "Don't you think? If the parents are for it, there's no way the administration can stand against them for long."

"I highly doubt *all* the parents are for it," I said. "I want to believe this is happening, that the Academy will be the first place to allow those who are different to mingle and learn with the humans, but I just don't see it. I'm sure there are plenty of parents who want to maintain the integrity of their elitism."

"It's such—" Brigitte cut herself off and pressed her lips into a thin line.

"Bullshit," I offered.

Brigitte let out a whoosh of breath. "I wasn't going to use that term."

"I know," I said. "That's why I did."

"It's just—" she began. "If I had been allowed to show all of who I am at school, think of all the good I could have done. Think of all the opportunities I would have had to learn from professors who weren't scared of me. I could be years past where I am today if I didn't have to hide my abilities to fit in with the other people in this city. I wouldn't have had to travel all the way to Atlanta in secret to find a mentor who could handle me."

"I know," I whispered. "You're preaching to the choir, here. But humans don't change their minds so quickly."

We fell silent for a moment. I could hear Samuel washing the dishes in the farmhouse sink I knew so well. Usually, that was my job after dinner. Maybe we should invite Samuel over more often.

"If there was a way to organize," Brigitte said, finally. "If we could get a petition started, and everyone in favor could put their name to it. All of us who would be thrown out if they knew what we were, what we could do, maybe we could stand together. Would you do that?"

I hesitated. Would I? Just the thought of it left a sinking feeling in my chest. It wasn't the part of me that was Potesta that worried. It was the part of me that called to the ocean. The part that could influence through words. The part that the humans feared more than anything on land. Could I reveal that?

"I don't know," I said.

Brigitte's face fell. Surely she could understand where I came from. Surely she could see how it was different for me.

"Well, think about it," she said. "There's no guarantee it's going anywhere anyway."

I nodded and took another sip of my water. No guarantee, sure, but if the parents were starting to push... Once that dam opened, there would be no stopping the deluge that would unfold. It could easily split the Academy in half.

Or more than that.

That kind of tumult could destroy the Academy entirely.

Chapter Four

Bang, bang, bang, click.

Reload. Bang, bang, bang.

I stripped the magazine out of my gun with my right thumb, already preparing the second one in my left hand to drive it into the weapon. Samuel stood beside me; his ear protection clamped heavily over his ears. Yellow-tinted glasses cast a sickly pallor over his dark face. His eyes focused downrange at the target as I loosed three more shots.

Samuel had started teaching me to shoot as soon as I was on my feet again after the Bettencourt case. My hands ached from the recoil and an ugly callous was forming in the palm of my right hand. But I didn't complain, as much as I wanted to. I knew that this weapon was my best bet against anything this city had to offer.

"Very good," Samuel said. "I think most of them landed on the target this time."

I could hear the laughter in his voice. I made a grimace and hit the button on the wall to bring the target toward us. The paper target ran on a metal track, its bottom-half flapping in the air as it zoomed toward us. It came to a stop an arm's length in front of me. And he was right, again. My grouping wasn't tight enough. Most of the shots landed on the paper, but very few on the torso silhouette that was printed on the target.

"You're making that face again," Samuel said.

"I am not," I told him before schooling my face blank.

Samuel ran a hand down his cheek as he surveyed my handiwork. "You know, I expected that in three weeks of work, you'd get better at this."

A sound that was remarkably close to a growl emerged unbidden from my throat.

I dropped the magazine out of the pistol I held, catching it in my left hand and placing it on the table before me. I cleared the chamber and set the safety before placing the gun beside it. That part at least I knew how to do. That part Dad had shown me when my hands were just barely large enough to hold a gun. He hadn't taken me to a range or taught me how to shoot when I was three. But he made damn sure I knew how to handle a gun safely if I ever came across one. To disarm it and clear the chamber. To get away from one safely.

I stared at the pistol that lay before me. It was a standard issue service weapon. The kind the NOPD carried. Samuel brought it with him each time we met up at the range. I was relatively sure it was the only kind of gun he'd ever used. After the way he left the NOPD, I would have assumed he'd want to replace the weapon with something else, but no. The gun he let me practice with, and the one he used in the lane beside me most days, were 9mm, standard issue, Glock.

"What do you need to adjust to get a tighter grouping?" Samuel prompted.

I wracked my brain to figure out what he wanted to hear. He'd told me something recently about how to group my shots tighter. What was it? I squinted at the paper target.

I couldn't remember, maybe I should listen to him more often.

"Do you think I should keep my eyes open when I pull the trigger?" I asked sweetly.

"You're closing your eyes?" Samuel exclaimed. He paused as he saw my face. "You're teasing me."

"I'm teasing you," I said.

Samuel cleared his throat. "If you look over here, most of your shots are grouping up to the right of the target. That tells me that when you pull the trigger, you're pulling it sideways. Your trigger motion should be front to back, if you're tugging to the side, you'll miss the target completely."

"Or I could just shoot to the left of my target," I teased. "That would work too, wouldn't it."

"Or you could just learn to shoot properly," Samuel said.

"Aye aye, captain."

Samuel turned me, warm hands on my shoulders. "This is serious, Meranda. Try to pay attention."

I gave him my widest eyes.

Samuel frowned. "Close your eyes," he said.

I did so automatically.

"Hold out your hands."

I held them out, palm up. This wasn't the first time we'd done this exercise. A weight settled in each of my hands. Cold metal against my palms.

"Now tell me which magazine contains silver bullets," Samuel said.

I hefted the magazines in my hands, testing their

weight. The one in my left hand was heavier but—I drew my eyebrows together. This wasn't like last time.

"Too late," Samuel interrupted my thoughts. "You're dead."

"That's not fair," I said. "You filled them with a different number of bullets. Just because one's heavier doesn't mean it's the silver one."

"You need to learn how to make this call in any situation," Samuel said. "You're not always going to have the time or the visibility to figure out which is which. This should be automatic, ingrained. You need to be right or you're dead."

I made what I was sure was an ugly face and set the magazines down.

"Do you think a shifter is going to wait for you to count how many bullets are in your magazine, Meranda?"

I bit back a retort and shook my head.

"A werewolf could cross the length of this range in less than thirty seconds," Samuel said. "He could shift into his hybrid form in less than three seconds, and he can do it mid run. He's not going to give you a chance to get your wits about you before he rips your throat out with one claw."

My sarcasm couldn't sit idly by while I was being lectured. "One claw? Really?" I asked. "You don't think maybe he'd use more than one? They're all attached to the same paw anyway, aren't they? I think maybe he'd use more than one."

"This is serious, Meranda," Samuel said. He crossed his arms, and I tried not to laugh. I found him positively hilarious when he was trying to be serious.

Tension stretched between us, the air thick with it. It strained at my chest. I'd gone too far. Samuel turned and began packing the pistols into their cases. I knew the next step was to take them back to the Agency and clean them.

I grabbed his forearm as he placed the last gun case into his dark blue backpack.

"Maybe you don't think I'm taking this seriously because you and I have a different view of the non-humans in this city," I said.

Samuel frowned. The lines pulled around his mouth. Dark ravines in his face.

"You assume anything that doesn't look like you is a threat," I said slowly. "I don't think that's entirely your fault. That comes from your training, and it comes from what you've seen. But *I* know that any shifter I meet on the street is as likely to help me as he is to harm me. I've had plenty of friends and assets who didn't spend a full moon's night in human form. You forget that I'm also the stuff of nightmares to the humans in this city."

The lines deepened on his face, and I dropped my tone. "Maybe this constant drilling of what a silver bullet would feel like in my hand reveals a bit of a bias in you. I'm not sure it will serve you in our line of work."

"I can teach you how to shoot," Samuel said, turning away from me. "I can't teach you how to think."

I followed him out of the range, glaring daggers into his back. Well, at least I tried.

Chapter Five

"Miss Haley."

I looked up from the papers I had been putting into a folder. Lucia Bonet stood before me; her petite formed dwarfed by the backpack she wore. Her fingers tangled in the black curls that hung to her chest. Dark eyes peered at me from her pale face, questioning.

"Yes, Lucia, did you need something?"

The rest of the class filed out behind her. She looked over her shoulder until the last of them had exited the room before she spoke again. "Miss Haley, I know you've said that the Rift wasn't something that we have to worry about anymore. But I am worried." She shuddered. "I keep having dreams about it. Nightmares that something else is going to crawl out of it. Something that we can't fight off."

I pushed the folder aside and clasped my hands atop my desk. I gave her what I hoped was my most non-worried face.

"Lucia, when the Sarduun first crawled out of the Rift, we didn't know what it was. We had never seen one before.

It's been a quarter century since we finally pushed it back from whence it came. We haven't seen anything like it since."

"Yes, but we didn't destroy it," Lucia insisted. "You just said we pushed it back to wherever it came from, but it's not dead. It could come back, couldn't it?"

Her worry tugged at something deep in my chest. It was a worry I shared. She was young. So young. But I couldn't tell her a lie. "The Potesta were created to keep us safe from the spirits. There are plenty of them still around. Plenty who haven't died in the last twenty-seven years since their creation. I'm sure if ever something arises from the Rift, we will have plenty of help taking care of it."

Lucia didn't look entirely convinced.

"You can't forget the gift the Sarduun gave us before it left. Your parents told you about that, didn't they?"

"The spirit scared our enemies away too," Lucia said. "It scared the melusine back to their watery depths. Back to their frigid city beneath the waves."

I gave her a smile, a gentle smile I hoped. "That's right. The melusine were vulnerable to attack from the Sarduun, just as the humans were. I don't want you to forget that the humans were losing that war. When Lo'tan rose with his army of melusine, they were stalking across this land. The city almost fell. Even with reinforcements from Atlanta and from Texas, there was no guarantee that we were going to win." I swallowed the word "we". It was hard for me to say.

Lucia gave a little shiver. "And what's to stop *that* from happening again?"

Had I just replaced one fear with another? Damn, I was bad at this.

I thought through my next words, watching her face as I spoke. "There's no guarantee of anything in this life; it's important that you remember that. But I also know that this city is doing everything it can to keep you safe from what it deems to be a threat."

"Like the shifters?" Lucia drew her eyebrows together, a tiny wrinkle forming between them.

"Your parents and the leaders of this city are doing what they think is best," I said.

"But you," Lucia asked. "Do you think the shifters are a danger to us?"

I stared at her for a long moment. She fidgeted slightly under my gaze. I knew I was being intense, but there was something about her question that made me draw short.

"What do you think about the shifters, Lucia? We'll say it's a teacher-student discussion. Your parents don't need to know what you say here."

"I don't think they're all that bad," Lucia said. "I have seen them before, like in the city, I mean. They don't scare me."

"You've seen them before," I asked.

Lucia shrugged. "Maybe more than seen them."

"You have a friend who's a shifter," I prompted gently, as gently as I could.

Lucia gave me a sheepish smile. "I might."

I smiled. "I have friends who are shifters too."

"It's being discussed—" Lucia paused. I held my silence, giving her the space to continue at her own pace.

"I've heard that maybe they're talking about allowing shifters into the school. Allowing fae into the school..."

"I don't know, Lucia," I said. "I'm not in charge of these decisions."

Lucia rolled her shoulders back and tightened the straps on her backpack. "Well, if they do allow them in," she said, "I don't think it would be such a bad thing."

I sat back in my chair. "I don't think so either."

Lucia gave me a small smile.

"I'll see you tomorrow, Miss Haley."

"See you tomorrow," I murmured.

I sat still for a moment as she left, letting the conversation wash over me. Maybe things were going to change around here. Maybe I would be teaching a classroom full of were-cats next semester. I shook myself. Probably not though.

I drew the keyboard on the desk toward myself. I had work to do. If the internet at the Agency was up and running, I could do it there. But that wouldn't be possible today.

I was done teaching for the day. This classroom wouldn't be used again until the morning. I had plenty of time.

Maybe if I knew more about our employer, about what he handled, maybe I could better understand what we were looking for. I pulled up a search database and typed in our employer's name: Janus Poincare.

As soon as I hit enter, I knew I was on the wrong path. Every single article was about his philanthropic works. How much good he did for the city. How much income he brought in each year. Income from what?

I tried a different tactic. I typed in the address of the office where we had first met. It was a nice office, glass doors and art on the walls that probably cost more than my house.

Whatever he did. It made him plenty of money.

The search results populated. The address was an acquisitions firm for museums. That was odd. Most museums had foregone accepting new acquisitions by now. Other than the ship exhibit that the school visited the day before, most exhibits were cycled from existing artifacts. It was too dangerous to bring relics of a bygone age across the wilderness to the city. Rangers could keep people safe on the crossing, but they were expensive, and it was no guarantee.

I scrolled through a list of services the acquisitions office offered. One word caught my eye: artifacts. Specifically, island artifacts.

Anything acquired from the islands in the Caribbean had to be smuggled into town. New Orleans Police Department didn't look too kindly on people bringing banned items into the city. I had a feeling that whatever we were dealing with was something less than legal. It didn't bother me much to work such a case, but it sure did explain why our client didn't go to the police first.

I typed in the code that Dad had given me long ago. It enabled me to search databases that were hidden from the average user. Oleksandr's eyes had bugged out of his head the first time he saw me use it. I don't know where Dad had gotten it, but wherever it was, Oleksandr didn't think I should have it. I put the word 'missing' before 'artifacts' and reduced the search parameters to the last few months. A list of amulets, necklaces, and broaches appeared on the screen. I scrolled through them. There was no real consensus what this item might be. No search result displayed in neon letters 'Mr. Poincare is looking for this specific broach'. I was basically where I had started.

"I don't think that's what you're looking for." A voice beside my shoulder made me jump.

I turned in my chair so quickly I almost fell out of it. Leaning close to my shoulder was the stranger. The one from Baxter's, the one who had been at the museum yesterday. His blue eyes were fixed on the screen of my computer. He wasn't looking at me, but the smirk on his face told me that he was absolutely aware of how much he'd startled me.

"You're following me," I said, shortly.

The stranger laughed. It was a deep sound. Almost a chuckle. It pulled at something in the pit of my stomach. It was a good laugh.

"It's not all about you, Meranda," he said.

I gestured at the computer screen. "How do you know that's not what I'm looking for?"

The stranger straightened. All six feet of him towered over my chair. He leaned back against the wall, as though he didn't mean to stand over me. He just wanted to have a conversation.

"Let's just say, I have experience with this sort of thing," he said. The sun streaming in the window played over the light stubble on his cheeks coloring some of the blond hairs almost silver.

"Experience with missing artifacts or smuggling?" I asked.

"We don't know each other well enough for you to get that answer," he said. A flash of white teeth followed.

I folded my arms across my chest and crossed my legs. "If you're not following me, then what are you doing here?"

"That," he said, pushing off the wall and turning toward the classroom door, "is none of your business."

I sprang from my chair and stood in the doorway. I watched his back as he walked up the hall. Did no one in this school care that a complete stranger was among the students? The hall was empty as classes had resumed sessions, but still. I saw Master Harnock at the end of the hallway. His feet planted shoulder-width apart, his arms folded. His expression was stony, but that was the way he always looked.

Surely, he would do something. Surely, he would know that this man was too young to have students at this school. I was just waiting for Harnock to reach out a hand and grab the stranger. He would throw him out on the street, maybe even demand his name from him. I'd like that.

Harnock raised a hand. I cocked my head to one side. It wasn't to throw the stranger out. It was to greet him. The stranger stepped forward and they clasped arms. Oh, shit. They knew each other.

I turned back to my classroom. You can bet Harnock and I would be discussing that at our next combat training.

The image results page was still on my monitor. It stared at me. Useless. It wasn't safe to work here anyway. I shut down the computer and pushed the keyboard back in front of the monitor before lining the mouse up beside it. A quick survey of the room told me that no student had left any belongings behind. I shut off the lights and locked the door as I left.

I had plenty to think about on my way to the Agency.

Chapter Six

My desk at the Agency was normally organized into a strict piling system. It wasn't tidy, but it at least had some degree of order. Today, a mound of crumpled sticky notes grew beside me. I'd been trying to get the Internet up and running for the last hour with no luck. I had paid the bill over the phone, determined to be able to work from my office even if it meant taking out a second mortgage on the house to make it happen. The impossibly saccharine voice on the phone assured me that, 'everything should be working, dear. Must be a problem on your end,'.

I decided I better stop trying before I threw the keyboard across the room. Maybe I could call Oleksandr. It's not really his expertise, but maybe he could offer some advice.

Samuel lay on the couch across the room, eyes closed, looking as comfortable as anything. He'd spent the last half hour tracking down his contacts from the NOPD and calling in favors from friends to get us a lead on Poincare. His steady breathing told me that he was happy to settle in and wait for results. I considered throwing a balled-up sticky note at him.

It seemed to me that most of NOPD considered him a total pariah at this point. His years of service forgotten in the shadows cast by the tragedies surrounding his leaving. I had my doubts any informants he still had contact with would have something useful to say.

I rose from the desk. I needed to relax my nerves and the empty coffee cup beside me wasn't going to help.

Florentina had just finished a reading as I left the office. The heavy mauve drapes of her parlour fell closed behind her customer as he left.

I drew up short.

The damn stranger who followed me was standing in my hallway. His blue eyes found mine, a half-smirk pulled at the corner of his mouth.

"No," I said.

"Again," he said, "I'm not here for you."

Before I could say anything else, he turned and ducked out the front door.

I tried to quell the feelings of frustration that rose in my chest. I wanted to scream. How could he not be following me? He was at my school this morning, for shit's sake. I blinked at the closed door. Or maybe I'd imagined him. That had to be it. It was too weird to have my nameless shadow in my hallway.

I made my way toward the kitchen at the end of the hall before I could do something really dumb like follow him.

Florentina was just placing a pot for hot water on the stove top as I walked in. The strings of white beads around her neck, clacked together as she lit the stove.

"Tea, dear?" she asked me.

I leaned against the counter. "Whatever you've got. Hopefully something relaxing."

"Case isn't going well." Florentina frowned, the lines in her weathered face deepening.

"Case isn't going at all."

Florentina turned toward me, the swish of her wide skirts a comforting sound against the cupboard behind her. "Maybe something else will take your mind off your troubles."

"Something else?"

"I know you took the case because the Agency needs the money."

I pushed off the counter and took a seat at the kitchen table. She was right, but I hated to hear it.

Florentina tracked my movement. "What if I found another case for you? Something you could solve quickly. Maybe you wouldn't be under so much stress to finish this one. Have some income to tide you over, maybe?"

"What case?" My skin itched. I wanted to dive into a bayou, wash off the stress.

"Oh, just something that came up," Florentina said. "Someone who came to me for a reading. I think maybe he could benefit from your expertise."

"Sarcasm and bitterness?"

"No, Potesta."

The smile fell from my lips. So, it was ghosts then.

"I can't guarantee anything," I said. "Give me his name and phone number. I'll see if I can get ahold of him."

Florentina smiled. A wide brilliant smile. She'd known I would agree. "Oh, you must have seen him as you walked in here, dear," she said. "He was just leaving."

"You've got to be kidding me."

Florentina chuckled softly. "He said you might react

that way."

"Oh, did he?" I asked. My cheeks burned. "Did he tell you that he's been following me around this entire city for the past week?"

I couldn't explain this overwhelming fire that was rising in me. I hated that he was everywhere. I hated that he seemed to know so much about me when I knew next to nothing about him. It made me feel like the punchline to some twisted joke and we were just getting finished with the set up.

The teapot behind Florentina whistled. My aunt turned and poured the tea into two cups. The one she handed me was porcelain, painted with blue flowers and vines. It was almost as delicate as I felt at the moment. Infinitely shatterable.

"Perhaps it's the ghosts that are following him," Florentina said. "Maybe they draw him to you."

"Whatever it is," I said, "I'm getting really tired of it."

"Well, solve his problem," Florentina said. "Maybe he won't hang around anymore."

Was there a chance I was even considering this? Was I considering helping this infuriating man who dogged my steps? I brought the teacup close to my face and breathed in its warm scent. Raspberry washed over me.

"I'll think about it," I said. "Give me his information."

Florentina took a scrap of paper from the drawer beside the fridge. A spare pen labeled with the name of some conference Dad had gone to on informational technology came next. She scribbled down a name and phone number and passed it to me. I took a glance at it before shoving it in the back pocket of my slacks.

Nathaniel Lawrence.

Now, I had a name.

Chapter Seven

When I came back from the kitchen, Samuel informed me that none of his contacts came through. I didn't know if that meant forever or if they were still working on it. Either way, I knew we had to try something else.

I made the call.

We met at Baxter's despite Oleksandr's protestations. This time he only pointed out ten things he objected to in the entrance. The dark wooden floorboards were scuffed. The tables off center.

I think he was starting to warm up to the place.

We sat at my usual spot at the bar, with a good view of the mirror so I could watch my back. The barstool beside me, where Oleksandr tapped a message into his phone, remained empty in the reflection.

The rest of the bar wasn't too crowded. A few small groups meeting in the early afternoon. Baxter's was a neutral space. Charlie wouldn't let anything happen in this bar. I certainly wasn't in the mood for trouble.

I fished into the bowl of peanuts before me and sipped

at my beer. Ever since I started drinking again, Charlie seemed more than happy to let me sample anything he had on tap. This was a new one. It had more head than I was used to and left a warm oaky aftertaste on the back of my tongue.

I kept my shields up against the static. I wasn't drinking enough that I thought I would be vulnerable to the spirits on Bourbon Street, but still I maintained the barrier. It was good practice. The shields brought a strange numbness that seemed to pulsate around me. I wasn't used to holding them this way. It still took a good amount of effort, despite Florentina's lessons.

I glanced down the bar top. Baxter's dog bed lay empty. The bulldog's absence left a tangible emptiness in the room. I made a mental note to ask Charlie about it next time he walked up. I knew the dog was getting older, but so help me, if I had to go the rest of my life without that smooshy face drooling on my hand one more time, I would lose it.

Oleksandr finished whatever message was so urgent and gestured for me to speak.

He sat in silence as I explained the situation, but he made a tsking sound when I mentioned our client's name.

"You've dealt with him before?" I asked.

"I've heard of him," Oleksandr said, examining one straight cut fingernail on his right hand.

"Good things?" I asked.

"He's a good businessman," Oleksandr said.

I knew what that meant. If we didn't come through with the case, we were screwed.

"Well, do you have any suggestions for how we find out what he lost?"

Oleksandr twisted his barstool around and leaned back against the bar's surface, resting his elbows over the counter.

"I may have someone we could ask," he said. He looked me up and down. "You up for a walk?"

I looked down at my sensible black boots and brown slacks. They were light enough to keep me cool in the midday heat. Even in October, the days maintained their warmth this close to the Gulf.

"Let's go," I said.

I threw some money on the bar and waved to Charlie as we walked out the door. I'd have to ask about Baxter later.

Oleksandr opened his dark umbrella as we stepped out onto the street and lifted it over his head. I knew we made an odd picture walking down Bourbon Street in the October afternoon. He wore his typical dark slacks and black button up. His dark hair combed back; porcelain skin perfect. Expensive sunglasses sat atop his slim nose. And then there was me. Wrinkled blouse tucked into cheap brown slacks, black boots where you would expect dress shoes to be, brown hair pulled back into a ponytail that I had barely thought to smooth down before tightening the band.

He held out his elbow and I took it with my right hand. I wasn't about to be rude. His arm was cool beneath my touch, and hard. Not like ice, though, like well-toned muscle. As though if I pressed hard enough, it might ripple beneath my touch. I supposed, in that way, walking down the sidewalk, we looked just like a couple. The thought made me want to balk. I wondered if Oleksandr liked that.

His face was neutral, serene. Beneath that dark umbrella, he could have been any other pedestrian on the street. His fangs hidden behind his pale lips. He caught me staring and flashed me a smile. There were the fangs. I looked forward.

We walked through the New Orleans back streets.

Away from Baxter's; away from Bourbon Street. I didn't know where he was leading, but you can bet I was laying down mental breadcrumbs as we went. I'd be able to find my way back, wherever we ended up. I didn't believe that he was trying to get me lost, but we certainly ended up down alleys I didn't recognize. A voice in the back of my head asked if I trusted him enough to be following him this way.

I truly didn't.

I trusted him to be friendly. I trusted him to flirt and have a good time while we worked together. He would keep me safe so long as it suited him, I knew. And when it didn't suit him any longer, he'd drop me like a hot rock. I also knew that I didn't have another choice. We turned down a darker alley, away from the afternoon sun. The sudden darkness sent a chill through me. I hoped that keeping me around still suited him.

There was a knife tucked into my right boot. A four-inch blade with a serrated edge near the handle. In the small of my back, tucked into my waistband, I carried a switch blade. The loose blouse made sure no one would know it was there until I needed it. I caught myself clenching and unclenching my free hand as we walked. Readying myself for whatever danger might lie down this darkening way.

Oleksandr took down his umbrella and hooked it over his arm. I guessed we wouldn't be going out into the sun again anytime soon. We came to a stop before a nondescript door on the left side of the alley. Oleksandr knocked once, and I looked up the walls toward the top of the building. It was at least three stories tall, mostly concrete, some of it cracked in places. I snapped my eyes back to the door as a window in the center of it slid open and a blue-tinged face peered out.

"What do you want?"

Oleksandr slid the sunglasses down his nose and peered over them at the fae.

The fae's mouth curved into an 'O' of recognition and the window slid shut. I heard the distinct sound of at least six deadbolts turning before the door opened.

Immediately my senses were hit with the smell of spices, incense, and gunpowder. What was this place?

Oleksandr took my hand from his arm and gestured for me to enter before him. I stepped through the doorway, grateful that the alley was dark enough that my eyes didn't take long to adjust to the low light. Not that there was much to see. Just a short hallway, with light fixtures on the walls that wanted desperately to be mistaken for lanterns.

The hallway was strangely empty. It only led to a set of stairs. From the top of those steps, I realized, you could see all the way to the door we had come through. The entirety of the hallway would be in view. This was a funnel. If someone was coming through here, hell, if a whole army of someones was coming through here, it would be easy to defend and escape from the top of the stairs. That told me there had to be another exit from up there.

The lesser fae who let us in settled into his chair beside the door and snapped open a magazine. *Carrion Weekly* I read on the title. A picture of a platter filled with raw meat took up the cover space. Upon closer inspection, some of that meat still had beaks and claws attached. I turned away. Not something I needed to subscribe to.

"Shall we?" Oleksandr asked.

We walked up the worn wooden stairs. I could feel the

cold of his skin at my back. There was something comforting about it.

We'd worked cases together before I left my father's Agency to pursue my teaching license. Dad seemed to trust him without limits. I don't know what deal he and Dad had worked out, but he was always there when Dad needed him. I wondered if that agreement extended to me. He hadn't demanded payment for his help yet. Maybe that was coming.

At the top of the stairs was a small landing, just a few feet across. A left turn brought us onto a balcony. I stopped short. A well-muscled arm appeared before me blocking my access. Across the way, I could see an identical balcony. Below, on the main floor, were stalls and platforms and all the sounds of a bustling marketplace.

I stepped back as a body came into view, blocking out the light from the doorway. He stood at least seven feet tall with broad shoulders and a mane of hair that fell in dark coils down to the center of his back. A vest covered his otherwise naked torso, leaving dark curls of hair visible across his chest. He wore loose shorts on his bottom half, held up by a massive belt nearly the width of the kind I had seen Master Harnock use for weight training. The blade of an ax peeked up over the man's right shoulder, its hilt visible behind his left arm.

"Who are you," the man asked, his voice a deep rumble that nearly vibrated through me.

Before I could answer, Oleksandr was at my side. He drew me behind him as he stepped forward.

"It's okay, Dray," he said. "She's with me." There was no hint of defensiveness in his voice. No inclination that he was worried that this man wouldn't let us through.

Without even a second glance my direction, Dray gave

one grunt of acknowledgment and stepped aside. I got a view of his back as he turned away. Damn, that ax was half my height. The weight on it had to be astronomical.

Oleksandr drew me out onto the balcony with one hand lightly clasping mine. Once on it, I could see that it truly did wrap around the entire room. Staircases in each corner of the building led down to the main floor and halfway down the length of each side was a small alcove like the one we stood in. Four entrances, perhaps. I was sure there were more exits from the main floor. There was no way anyone was setting up shop in the bottom of a proverbial fish barrel.

I followed Oleksandr to the closest staircase on our right.

"Why did you send me first?" I asked. "You knew a guard was there to stop me, wouldn't it have been easier to go first yourself?"

Oleksandr gave me a sideways glance as we walked but didn't answer.

"You wanted to know if he'd recognize me," I said, realization dawning on me. "You wanted to know if I'd been here before."

Oleksandr gave me a half-smirk before starting down the stairs.

I shook my head. *What was this place?*

Once we reached the floor, I could see that the building was much larger than it had looked from the balcony. It was the kind of place you'd expect to see in a textbook on medieval times, as though there should be lanterns and torches lighting the market. Instead, a warm sunlight illuminated the stalls. Skylights in the ceiling let the light in, casting the whole scene in a strange golden glow. I sent a glance Oleksandr's direction, but he didn't move to raise his umbrella. The glass must be tinted somehow.

Purple curtains hung heavy on the first stall we passed. They looked remarkably similar to the ones which covered the entrance to Florentina's parlor. The shelves of the stall were lined with vials of colored liquid. Dyes maybe. Mostly obscured by a curtain at the back of the stall, I could see the edge of a doorway.

An exit.

I made note of it.

I kept close to Oleksandr as we walked between the vendors. We passed all manner of nice-smelling stalls that sold meat and spices, pie and pastries. Bad-smelling stalls that sold what had to be potions, the harsh scent of gun powder and sulfur making its way to the walkway. Fabrics and jewels, pearls and shells, anything you could possibly want to procure in a city that banned it was here in this room.

It struck me then the trust that Oleksandr was putting in me. Belief that I wouldn't take this information directly to the police department. To bring me here, he must know how poorly NOPD and I got along. It wouldn't surprise me if he knew that I also had things to hide from those who ruled this city.

We came to a stop before a stall whose shelves were lined with amulets. Gold, silver, iron. Necklaces, broaches, jewels that seemed lit from within, jewels that hummed if you got too close. I eyed the humming ones and kept my distance. I knew that that kind of sound usually preceded some small explosion, and I didn't want to be here when it went off.

"Wait here a moment," Oleksandr said. Before I could reply, he ducked into the covered space. I did my best not to cross my arms at his absence. A petite young woman with a jade green tint to her skin sat on a stool at the back of the stall. She eyed me with the same wariness I used on the amulets beside me. She had dark hair, a pronounced widow's peak, and a heart-shaped face. A pixie of some kind maybe.

As Oleksandr spoke a few words to the stall owner, I eyed those who passed by. Most of them didn't watch others too closely. I figured with whatever vetting system they had to get in here, most people knew not to ask questions of one another's business.

A trio of shifters walked past me, their self-assured strides and the glint in their eyes told me that they changed into *something*, but what, I didn't know. One of them gave a sniff my direction before turning to elbow his friend. I leveled my gaze on them. It wasn't that I was worried they were going to cause a scene here in the market. They'd have to be some real kind of stupid to do that near all these unstable amulets. But I also wasn't about to let them think I was an easy target. I made eye contact with each of them in turn. *Not prey,* I thought as loudly as I could. *Not prey.*

A slight noise from inside the stall drew my attention and I looked over in time to see Oleksandr waving me in. I glanced back once to see that the trio were moving on before I ducked into the stall. I was careful not to bump my head on the amulets hanging over the entrance.

I gave the pixie my most genial smile as I approached. "Meranda Haley," I said, holding a hand out.

"What relationship do you have with Mr. Poincare," the pixie asked. She had a thick accent to her voice. Deep south.

I took my hand back. "He's a client," I said. I didn't know how much I was supposed to reveal about our dealings. Oleksandr's face was impassive beside me.

"He's an ass, is what he is," the pixie said.

"Now, Tina," Oleksandr chided. "He's a businessman.

Just because you got the raw end of the deal, doesn't make him an ass."

The pixie's face crinkled into a sour look. "He's an ass if I say he is. He threatened that he would make sure I couldn't work anywhere in the city if I didn't give him what he wanted."

Oleksandr raised his arms at his side as though she had just proven his point. "Like I said, he's a businessman. He'll say what he needs to get what he wants."

I wasn't sure I liked what I was hearing about our client. I should have known before I took the case that this was going to be a problem. But with the Agency so far in the red and no other cases coming in, I hadn't had much choice in the matter.

"What did Poincare have you doing?" I asked.

The pixie focused on me. "He was bringing in some products from the Gulf, from the islands down south. I was supposed to do the pickup from the ship and deliver it to his warehouse."

"And in return," I asked.

"One of the items was mine," she said. Her pointed teeth flashed. Tiny white needles in her small mouth. "An amulet I needed."

"What happened?"

"Part of the cargo was missing."

I glanced at Oleksandr.

"I didn't do it," the pixie snapped. Her accent thickened when she was angry. "Despite what Poincare thought. Someone on the ship must have stolen it."

"And what did Poincare do?"

"He said since a fifth of what I owed him was missing, he would take away a fifth of what he owed me."

"He broke apart the amulet?" I asked.

Tina's eyes flashed at me. A tinge of color touched her round cheeks. "He gave me the amulet he had promised," she said. "He took away its power."

"Its power," I asked. "You can do that?"

Oleksandr spoke up beside me. "Some mages can render magical artifacts inert. Often it is only for a time. It takes immense training to learn how to do. Extremely expensive. I'm sure Poincare paid a fortune."

"So have you ever worked for him again?" I asked.

"After that?" Tina gave a harsh laugh. "No chance in hell. And you've got to be three kinds of dumb to be doing a job for him, too."

I bit back whatever my mouth wanted to retort before I could get myself into trouble.

"How long ago was this job?"

The pixie tossed her hair over her shoulder, the long dark length cascaded down to the center of her back. "Two weeks ago," she said.

Bingo. Whatever was on that ship had to be what Poincare had hired us to find.

"Did you ever find out what was missing from the shipment?" I asked. "Did you figure out who took it?"

Tina shook her head. "Never did."

Damn it. That would have been too easy.

"What was the name of the ship," I asked. "The one which had the missing cargo."

The pixie looked surprised that I cared, but she told me. "The *Star of the Sea*."

Progress.

"You didn't think to ask the captain or any of the crew what happened? Why something was missing?" I asked.

The pixie shrugged. "I hadn't known it was missing

until I got to the warehouse. By the time I even thought of going back to the docks, everyone was gone."

"And you just thought that Poincare wouldn't notice that some of the cargo never made it?"

Tina leaned back and crossed her arms over her chest. "Are you accusing me of something?"

I shook my head. "No, not at all. I wouldn't do that."

Something told me Poincare was better off never working with this pixie again. If someone I hired didn't do their due diligence to ensure that what they picked up was what they were *supposed* to pick up, I wouldn't trust them again either.

"Thank you for answering my questions," I said, almost turning to go.

The pixie gestured around her stall. "Aren't you going to buy something?"

I gave her the most pleasant smile I could muster. "Of course," I said. I should have known no information was free, whether I was with Oleksandr or not.

I turned in a small semi-circle around the stall. My eyes lit on a light blue crystal. It was only about two inches long, tapered to a point at the end. The sunlight that hit it cast rainbows of aquamarine around the stall. I knew just who would enjoy that.

"I'll take this," I said.

The pixie gave me a price that I was sure was a rip-off for what was probably a piece of glass, but I paid it anyway. With the name of the ship, she had given me a lead. I told myself I was paying for that.

Chapter Eight

Oleksandr offered me his arm again as we stepped out of the stall.

"You did great," he said. "You're a natural at this."

"It's not my first time interviewing someone," I said.

"No, but you're out of practice." His voice was smooth and rich, like a fine bourbon.

We walked together in silence for a moment before Oleksandr spoke again.

"Do you have an artifacts expert who can help you? With the dangerous nature of what Poincare deals with, I'd hate to see something go wrong."

I shook my head.

"I know of one," he said. "And lucky for you, he's just come back to town."

"Can you arrange a meeting?" I asked. "I'd appreciate having the asset."

A fang flashed on the side of Oleksandr's mouth as he smiled. "Of course."

We made our way up what appeared to be the main

thoroughfare through the market. It was louder here, hawkers shouting their wares on either side of us. A booth holding live animals in cages caught my eye. I made the mistake of slowing in front of it and the scarred man just within the entrance called to me.

"You look like you could use a friend." An emerald-green constrictor draped over his shoulders, half of its mass trailing to the floor behind him as he moved forward. A jagged scar tore down his right cheek, pulling the eyelid half closed on that side.

I shook my head, but my feet had stalled to a stop at the sight of the snake coiling and uncoiling its length, seeming to draw tighter around the man's neck with each movement.

"Surely you'd like something..." he eyed me up and down, assessing me, personalizing his recommendation. "Scaly?"

Not hardly. I smiled and started to move away.

"Wait, miss," he called. "I meant fuzzy. A furry friend, a kell perhaps?"

"Nice try," I said. "I don't think—did you say a kell?"

Yellow teeth flashed at me under his scraggly mustache. "Yes," he said. "Yes, a kell. Not even imprinted yet. Come closer."

He stepped aside to reveal a cage in the middle of the stall. A gap in the cloth atop the stall let a sunbeam in, like a spotlight, on the animal inside. Its back was toward us as it lay on its side. It could have been a normal rabbit for all I knew from that angle.

I almost stepped inside the stall, very nearly followed the man in even though his eyes glowed with greed as he thought he'd found an eager customer. I stopped. What the hell would I do with a kell?

I raised a hand. "No, thanks."

The man's lips almost turned to a scowl before he schooled himself. "Very well ma'am," he said, again flashing those yellow teeth like blocks of dulled sidewalk chalk. "Come back if you need anything."

I returned to Oleksandr's side.

"A kell? Really?" the vampire asked. "That's what made you stop?"

"I have a bet going with Samuel," I said. "He thinks they aren't real. I say they are. Bringing one home seemed a good way to settle it."

"Well, if it's to prove Samuel wrong," Oleksandr said, "Let me buy it for you."

"Absolutely not," I said, tugging on his arm. "I don't even understand what the draw is to own an animal so dangerous it can kill you in seconds."

"Typically, there is no draw," Oleksandr said. To my relief he started walking again. "Unless they're unimprinted."

"The stall owner said this one is."

"Ah, then," Oleksandr said, as though that was explanation enough.

I was going to ask him to clarify when I spotted them.

The same trio of shifters I had seen before were walking up the aisle toward us. I drew Oleksandr to the side, half-hiding my body behind his. Something in their faces told me they were pissed and looking for an excuse to take it out on something. As the group passed, I saw one of them raise his upper lip, showing off a row of sharp teeth. Beside me, Oleksandr inclined his head to the group. It wasn't a demure gesture; it almost looked like a mocking challenge.

I wasn't sure what the rules were in this underground market, but I sure didn't want to find out what happened if a pissed off shifter tried to take on a vampire.

I pushed Oleksandr back between two of the stalls, into more of the shadows. The group of shifters carried on up the aisle.

"I'm not a child, Meranda," Oleksandr said. "I wasn't going to eat them."

"Maybe not," I said. "But they were looking for a fight. I'm not in the mood for trouble today. Not when I finally have a lead to work on."

"Are you ever in the mood for trouble?" Oleksandr purred.

I smacked my hand against his cold hard arm. "No. Most of the time, I just happen to be around when it happens."

Oleksandr's white teeth flashed in the shadows where we stood. "A bad habit of yours, I'm sure."

I poked my head out between the stalls. A commotion sounded to our left. I felt Oleksandr's chill radiating onto my arm as he stood beside me.

"It seems the werewolves found someone else to bother," he said, amusement in his tone.

"Let's go," I said. "No reason for us to get caught up in whatever chaos they're brewing."

I took one step forward and the stall beside us exploded into wooden splinters and shattered glass. Oleksandr twisted me around, taking the brunt of the explosion across his broad back. He grunted and leaned in against me. I wasn't sure how thick vampire skin was, but from the sting of one splinter that grazed my cheek, I knew his back must look like a set of porcupine quills.

Shit.

My hand was at the small of my back, almost automatically pulling out the compact switchblade and snapping it open. I looked over Oleksandr's shoulder through the space left from the demolished stall. The three werewolves in their hybrid forms stood toe to toe with a group of fae. Sparkles glittered around the faes' blue arms as they held them up, ready to cast their slight magic to defend themselves. Whatever had blown up the stall beside us had almost assuredly been cast by one of them.

Apparently, they had crappy aim.

I pulled on Oleksandr's arm. With the werewolves already given into their bloodlust, the last thing they needed to spot was a vampire. We had to get out of here before they saw us.

"You," the accusation came from the tense group.

I cursed the shifter and his pronounced sense of smell. All three of the werewolves turned toward us, the fae forgotten. They really were out for vampire blood. Did vampires bleed? I hoped I didn't get the chance to find out.

Oleksandr looked almost ready to step forward and take them all on himself, but I made a slight hissing sound behind him to remind him that I was still there.

"We don't want any trouble," Oleksandr said. His voice rang clear above the sounds of the market packing up around us. His back was toward me as he blocked my body with his frame. Only I could see as he reached his hand to the back of his waist band and pulled out a small pistol.

I wondered if he knew the feeling of silver bullets in a magazine.

The lead werewolf spoke again. "You insulted our friend."

Bullshit. "He did no such thing," I called out. I put my hand on Oleksandr's arm, stilling his movement. There had to be a way out of this without killing anyone.

The shifter beside the werewolf who had just spoken

stepped forward. "He's a vampire," he said. "His very existence is an insult."

Yeah, there was no way we were getting out of here without killing someone. Can't say I didn't try. I let go of Oleksandr's arm, turned, and ran up the aisle.

If Oleksandr had any sense, he would follow me. A few shots rang out behind me, but I kept going. I held the switchblade reversed in my palm, so the blade was flat against my forearm. I would be damned before I'd accidentally stabbed myself while I ran. The blade had a silver tip, but its length was mostly steel. I didn't imagine the small amount of silver would actually hurt a werewolf enough to stop them before they tore me apart. A howl sounded behind me, and I drove my legs harder. I didn't want to find out.

A shimmering sound came from behind and I threw myself to the ground. My chin scraped the floor of the aisle, and I tucked my arms around my head. The heat from the fireball bathed me as it passed overhead and slammed into a stall in front of me. I guess the fae weren't taking the chance to stay out of the fight. I spared a glance back the way I'd come. The fae couldn't be shooting at me, could they? I couldn't believe their aim really was that bad.

I rolled to the side as a swarm of fiery darts came soaring my direction. My body came to a stop between two carts. Not that they were much protection from the fire being thrown around here, but at least I was out of sight for a moment. Fae typically weren't powerful enough to sustain this kind of fire power. Someone else had to be involved.

I could only see a narrow slice of the main thoroughfare between the carts where I hid. A mage dressed in a red cape stepped out from the stall beside me and started up the main aisle, coils of lightning winding up his forearms.

It occurred to me then that maybe the peace in this market wasn't so well attended to. Maybe everyone in this underground space was just itching for a fight.

A grunt of pain and the mage flew back through my line of sight. His body crashed into the ground and slid unmoving out of view.

I scrambled to my feet as a werewolf came around the corner. His eyes practically glowed gold as he sought me out. He had to be close to six and a half feet in hybrid form. His hands tipped with claws the length of my palm; fangs visible on his snout.

"You smell like the bloodsucker," he growled.

I kept the switchblade hidden from view in my right hand as I held up my left.

"We're acquaintances," I said. Diplomacy was always a good option, right?

The shifter took a step forward, but I stood my ground. He looked confused for a moment that I wasn't running away from him. I had run before. Six werewolves would kill me. But the thing was, one werewolf, I might be able to manage.

"*Stop*," I poured my power into my voice, seeding it with the gifts of my parentage.

The furrowed brow deepened on the face before me, but his feet halted.

"*Three steps back*," I told him, pushing forward with three steps of my own. "*The bloodsucker is that way.*"

Something in the shifter's eyes told me there was a fight going on in his head. Shifters were harder to compel than humans. It would be almost impossible to force him to do something that he absolutely was opposed to. I took the chance that he wanted Oleksandr more than he wanted to tear into me. It was just a nudge my siren's call gave him. A suggestion.

The shifter backed at my advance. I had him.

As soon as he hit the main thoroughfare, I was going to turn and run. That was my plan. It was a damn terrible one, but it was mine.

I didn't have to. The shifter's feet stumbled out into the main aisle and a whistling sound started. I leapt back as a fireball crashed into the werewolf's torso, engulfing him in flame and sending him flying somewhere to my left.

Damn.

I startled as Oleksandr landed beside me.

"You having fun yet?" His eyes glittered with excitement. I patted out a smoldering piece of his dress shirt, just over his left shoulder. It stung my hand, but I got the sparks out. Whoever was shooting the fireballs seemed to have the other two werewolves well-occupied.

I turned to Oleksander. "Don't you have claws and fangs and shit?"

"Of course."

"You still carry a gun?"

"You don't?" he asked.

Don't tell Sammy, I thought. "Just get me out of here."

Oleksandr pointed toward the wall behind me. There was room between the backs of the stalls and the side of the building. I squeezed my way through and ran as fast as the small space would allow until I reached the stairs. I looked up at them. There was no way in hell I was going up that railed staircase and painting myself a nice target to anyone who was watching.

I grabbed Oleksandr's hand and pulled him behind the first cart we had seen, the one that sold the cloths and dyes, to the door behind. I shoved against the door and nearly bounced off. Dammit. Oleksandr backed me up a step before turning and landing his right foot directly beside the handle. The door exploded outward into a dark alleyway, and I didn't stop. I ran directly toward the first patch of sunlight I could see and what I hoped was the protection of a pack of witnesses.

Oleksandr was right on my heels and the minute we broke out into the open air of a main street he let out a sharp hiss. Shit. He'd dropped his umbrella.

I pushed him back against the cool side of a building, where there was still a half a foot of shadow. It kept the sun out of his face anyway. Redness was already spreading across his forehead.

"Dammit, Oleksandr," I said. "Don't you wear sunscreen?"

"With the amount of oils and grease in it?" Oleksandr drew himself upright with all the grace of a ripening tomato. "Not a chance."

I had layered a black tank top under my blouse. It wasn't necessarily for occasions like this, but it worked. I stripped my shirt off and threw it over his head.

"Let's go," I said.

Oleksandr paused. His eyes trailed over my torso.

"What?" I looked down at my tanned arms. Swimming in the bayou had lengthened and toned my muscles.

"You look good," he said. A flash of white teeth under the shadow of my shirt.

"Shut up," I said.

I took his cool hand in mine and led him back toward Bourbon Street. With his face half-hidden under the blouse, he couldn't see the way we were going. I thanked the universe that I had remembered to mark my steps.

The first place we could find to buy an umbrella, we

were stopping. The cream blouse that shrouded Oleksandr's face carried scorch marks now, but I was sure I could get them out.

With the Agency so far in the red, I couldn't afford to destroy clothing right now.

Chapter Nine

I sat in a generic cafe on an unassuming street just south of the Agency, the Agency laptop open before me. The cafe wasn't my first choice, but they had free internet and decent coffee so here I was.

I dropped Oleksandr off at the first shop I saw that had even the barest chance of selling an umbrella. He'd declined to give me my blouse back in case he couldn't find the perfect umbrella to suit his needs. I grumbled at him, but I didn't have time to stick around and fight. Before I left, he pressed a piece of paper into my hand, a ten-digit number on it. No name. Super helpful.

There was no chance I was calling that number he gave me, his magical expert, until I'd done my own research.

I started with the most basic searches, typing in the name of the ship, hoping I could get the captain's name or information on how to book their services. It seemed that whoever owned *The Star of the Sea* didn't want it to be found. Not through normal means anyway. I understood that.

When I had exhausted even the most esoteric means I had of tracking the ship's captain down, I used the only resource left. I pulled out the piece of paper that Oleksandr had given me and made the call.

The ice cubes in my coffee clinked against each other as I took a sip. I listened to the phone ring on the other end. There was a hint of caramel in the roast, just bitter enough to taste like it was doing good work. None of the fancy sugar stuff for me. Not if I wanted to function for the rest of the day without shaking. Something about it threw off the salt in my blood. The phone rang longer than I expected before it was finally picked up.

"Hello?" the voice asked.

I almost cursed.

Even through the phone I recognized his voice. Deep and strong, like the coffee I swirled in my glass. *Why on earth hadn't Oleksandr just told me his name?*

"Nathaniel Lawrence," I said. "Meranda Haley."

"Meranda." I could hear a smile slide into his voice. "I was expecting your call."

Expecting my call? Oh shit, Florentina's thing. He thought I was taking his case. Dammit, dammit, dammit.

"Madame LaMontagne said you were looking for my help," I said.

"I can't pay you much," he said. It was the first time his voice didn't sound as though he was half flirting with me.

Can't pay. Great. Florentina had lied about that too.

"We can discuss the fees later," I said. "Why don't you meet me at the Agency in, say, a half hour? We can go over the specifics then."

"I'll see you there, Meranda." His voice lingered on my name. I wasn't sure if I liked that breathy sound he used, but I didn't entirely hate it either. I hung up the phone and took a deep breath. Something in my chest settled funny, not heavy, but off somehow. Shit. If him saying my name caused this reaction over the phone, what would it be like working with him in person.

I closed the laptop and dropped it into the messenger bag I had slung over the chair beside me. The ice in my cup rattled as I took one last drag of my coffee. I tossed the plastic cup into the trash on my way out the door. If I was going to be meeting with a client, I needed to find a new shirt.

Samuel wasn't at the Agency when I got back. He hadn't been there when I picked up the laptop either. I didn't know where he was, but hopefully he was tracking down a lead. He'd tell me when he had something.

Florentina was rearranging her parlour as I walked in. She tended to do that before readings to prepare for her client's specific needs. Or their specific weaknesses, I supposed. Today her card reading table was against the window. Light coming through the scarlet shades cast a red glow over the white lace tablecloth.

I didn't ask any questions, but I raised a hand in greeting as I walked by.

"I'm meeting with a client across the hall," I said, giving her the heads up so she'd know not to interrupt.

Florentina's brown eyes seemed to sparkle as she looked up from the card deck she was unpacking. "Sounds good, dear."

She knew. She knew who was coming. How the hell did she always know?

I turned on my heel and walked across the hall into my

dad's old office. His name was still on the door: Collier Investigations. I couldn't change it. Not yet. Not even with him gone.

My thoughts turned to his apartment upstairs.

I should visit him.

I set my satchel on the desk beside the useless computer. The drawer at the top of the desk held everything I might need. A notebook, some pens, a business card with my phone number on it.

The bell jingled on the front door, and I looked at the clock on the far wall. He was ten minutes early. An unladylike grumble started in my chest. I was normally punctual, but this was pushing it. I stepped out to the hall to greet him just as Florentina was coming out of her parlor. He stood for a moment looking between the two of us before a slight dimple showed beneath the blond scruff on his cheek. His eyes were a bright blue, like sunlight off the ocean. I shook myself out of my staring.

"Thanks for coming," I said. "Right this way."

Florentina stopped me with a slight gasp. "Oh, you can't meet in there!"

"Why not?" I asked, giving her the best shut up look I could muster.

"With all the renovations your office is undergoing, there's no way you can meet in there."

Renovations? What the hell?

"Oh, you must go upstairs," Florentina said.

To Dad's apartment?

Our client looked confused. I didn't blame him. I was confused.

I didn't know what game Florentina was playing, but I had trusted her my whole life, I wasn't about to stop now.

Dad had met clients in his front room before. To Florentina's point, the couch upstairs was much more comfortable than the beat up one in Dad's office.

I gave Nathaniel a slight shrug and gestured toward the end of the hallway. He passed me on the way to the stairs and I gave Florentina a questioning look.

"Is that what you're wearing?" she hissed.

I looked down at the crumpled band t-shirt I wore over my brown slacks. It was all I'd had in the car. At least I had washed the soot and dirt off my face from the market stall exploding beside me.

I didn't answer my aunt.

It had been polite to let Nathaniel advance before me, it was my Agency and he was a guest, but it sure made for an odd situation when he reached the top of the stairs and I needed to come up beside him to unlock the door to Dad's apartment.

He pressed back against the wall of the stairwell to give me space, but still my shoulder brushed against his chest as I leaned forward to access the doorknob. The thin shirt he wore was no barrier to the heat that radiated off him. The waves of it bathed my skin. I unlocked the door and pushed it open before I found out if he would burn me.

I felt my father's presence as we entered. He didn't show himself, but he was there.

"Can I get you some water," I asked. Ever the polite hostess.

Nathaniel shook his head and took a seat on the leather couch. I dropped down into an armchair across from him. "So, tell me what's going on."

Nathaniel settled in against the couch cushion and threw his arm over the back of the couch seat beside him.

He was entirely too damn comfortable in my father's apartment. I kept my face pleasant.

"I have a ghost problem." He said it nonchalantly, the way someone might mention having an off day. "Florentina said you could help."

"It's the sort of thing I handle," I said. "What kind of a ghost problem?"

"I'm being haunted."

"Everywhere?" I asked. Usually, ghosts are tied to a specific place, not so much a specific person. It was rare for them to change locations to follow someone.

"Everywhere in this city," he said.

"I hear you just returned to the city," I said. "When you were here before, were they following you then?"

Nathaniel smiled. It was a pleasant enough smile, but it didn't reach his eyes. The blue there darkened, calculating, as though he was trying to figure out what he could get away with not sharing.

"If you want my help," I said. "You have to be honest with me. I can't help you if you lie to me."

Nathaniel spoke slowly, as though he was choosing his words one by one. "When I was last in the city, I didn't stay long enough for them to find me."

"And when you left," I asked. "Did you go far?"

Nathaniel straightened and looked behind him. I could feel Dad's presence over his shoulder, but he still didn't show himself.

"What's in your apartment," he asked.

"Oh, that's just Dad," I said. "He's around. It's his apartment."

Nathaniel brought his arm back to his lap. He looked a little less relaxed on Dad's couch. I liked that better.

"Do you have any idea who this ghost might be?" I asked, trying a different line of questioning.

"I hate to say it, but it's kind of a long list."

I raised an eyebrow. That was interesting.

"Were you in a dangerous line of work?" I asked. "You saw a lot of death? Ranger, maybe?"

Nathaniel shook his head. "Not quite."

I remembered what he said back at the Academy when he saw what I was looking up on the computer. He knew about illegally procured artifacts. "The opposite, then."

Nathaniel met my eyes; his own blue were calm and still as a sea without wind. "The opposite, then," he whispered.

That whisper sent a chill up my spine. It spoke to something deep in the back of my head. Curled around me like a memory I couldn't quite grasp.

"I'll take your case," I said, the wheels already turning in my head. "Let's talk fee."

Nathaniel raised his shoulders in a slight shrug. "Like I said, I don't have much to pay you. Work hasn't been too frequent."

"I think maybe you have something else I need," I said. "Something other than money."

Nathaniel's eyes drifted toward my chest. He opened his arms and uncrossed his legs, the dark pants stretching to a lighter color on his thighs. "Whatever you need," he said. His voice was dark and low.

A flush flew onto my cheeks before I could stop it. "No, not that. Definitely not that. No," I said, my voice nearly stammering in my haste to stop him. "You said you had experience with artifacts, amulets and shit. That's the expertise I need."

Nathaniel gave me a smirk before bringing his legs

closer together. Dammit, he knew exactly what he was doing.

"Did you lose one of those?" he asked.

"A client of mine might have," I said.

"And if I help you find your amulet, you'll help me with my ghost problem?"

"That's the deal."

Nathaniel looked around the small apartment. "Is there a contract of some kind I need to sign?"

I stood up. "Or you could shake my hand," I said.

Nathaniel rose and extended an arm towards me. I took his warm calloused hand in my own. Whatever work he did must involve some manual labor. His hand was rough against mine. His grip was strong, but I responded in kind. One of the first things Dad taught me was how to shake a hand.

"So, what is it you're looking for?" Nathaniel asked.

"That's the problem," I said. "We don't know."

"Okay," Nathaniel said slowly. "You took a case without knowing what it was you were supposed to find?"

I didn't tell him we needed the money. I didn't tell him that I also was doubting that we ever should have taken on the case.

"That's where you come in," I said sweetly.

Nathaniel gave a light laugh. It resounded in my chest, tapping there against my heartbeat.

"Tell me what you have so far," he said, taking his seat again on the couch.

"A shipment of goods came in from the islands," I said. "About two weeks back. Something was missing off the shipment."

"Who's your client?" Nathaniel asked, that calculating look was back in his eyes.

"Janus Poincare."

A look of recognition crossed his face.

"You've worked with him before," I asked.

Nathaniel nodded once.

I felt Dad's presence, a cold prickle on the back of my neck. His spirit was behind me, watching Nathaniel over my shoulder. I hadn't yet told him about this case. Damn it, this was what Florentina had been playing at. She knew I had too much pride to admit to Dad that we took a case with a client he had avoided like the plague for decades.

Now that he knew, there was no way I could get out of telling him the details. I resisted the urge to throw a shield up between myself and his spirit. That wasn't fair. I tried to push some feeling of tentative apology toward him. I couldn't be sure if it came across.

"What else do you have?" Nathaniel asked.

"The name of the ship," I said. "*The Star of the Sea.*"

"Two weeks ago, you said?"

I nodded.

Nathaniel rose. "I'll see what I can find out."

"Thank you," I said and pulled a business card out of my back pocket. I handed it to him across the coffee table. Our fingers met for one moment as he took it from my hand. His warmth seeped into my bones, like sunlight on a shore.

"You call me," I said. "If you find anything. And you definitely call me if that ghost comes back."

"I will."

I held the door open for him and watched until he made it to the bottom of the stairs. He could find his way out.

Dad and I had to talk.

Dad's spirit stayed in the living room as I walked to the kitchen. I poured myself a glass of water from the tap and walked back, steeling myself for the conversation we were about to have. The couch cushions were still warm from Nathaniel's body. I sat anyway and drew my legs up.

I felt like nothing so much as a child again in my father's apartment, as though I was admitting to sneaking out and hanging out with a crowd I wasn't supposed to.

I was about to speak, to break the silence, when Dad's voice came from the space before me.

"I like him."

"He's a client," I said.

A smile was in the voice, a thoughtful tone. "I like him."

I could imagine my father nodding to himself as he spoke. Dad was being nice. He was easing some of the tension. Always so gentle.

"Are you disappointed?" My voice cracked.

The silence pressed on my chest. I could hardly breathe.

I took a shaky draw of breath. "Are you disappointed that I'm working with Poincare? I know you refused to work with him." I paused. "I think I'm starting to understand why."

A sigh sounded across the room. The silence stretched. He wasn't even replying. I blinked hard and took up my cup of water.

I walked back to the sink and rinsed out the glass before setting it in the strainer. The chilled silence hung on me like a wet cloak.

"I'll come back," I said. "We'll talk some more."

I had to go. I couldn't stay here in this heaviness when I'd hurt him so badly he wouldn't talk to me.

"Be careful," Dad's voice sounded. I stopped with one

hand on the doorknob and closed my eyes. It was almost like he was there, like he could put his arms around me and warm my chill. But he couldn't.

"I will."

I opened the door and left.

Chapter Ten

"Concentrate," Florentina snapped.

"I am concentrating," I said, screwing my face up at her. From where I sat at my kitchen table, my eyes closed, I could hear her huff of frustration. It had been two days since I set Nathaniel loose on our Poincare problem. No news is good news, right?

My ears picked out the clink of glasses on saucers as my aunt moved our tea dishes away.

"We should have had this squared away years ago." My aunt's Cajun accent deepened when she was frustrated, the words coming quick and clipped. The bangles on her wrists jingled together. She must have been talking with her hands again. Another habit that deepened in time with her emotions.

"Well, we didn't." I tried to keep my voice neutral. "So, let's make the most of what we have now."

"Fine, concentrate."

I stretched my powers out around me, like unfurling wings. I could feel the chill of Marie on the other side of the room, but I couldn't pinpoint her location. Usually, I used the visible clues around her, a paper fluttering beside her, a candle flickering, to figure out exactly where she was. With my eyes closed, it was like trying to feel texture through thick leather gloves. I'd relied on my external senses for far too long.

"Where is she now?" Florentina asked.

I pushed my power toward the chill, trying to differentiate bumps and ridges from the background static. "She's by the fridge."

"That is hardly specific, girl."

I pressed the pads of my fingers against my eyelids, blocking out any light that might tempt me to rely on them. My eyebrows furrowed, brushing against my fingertips.

"She's within five feet of the fridge," I said.

"Five feet," Florentina repeated. I had a feeling if she had a ruler, she would have rapped me with it. Note to self, never give Tante Flora a ruler.

A cool breeze tickled my skin, a light laugh from my resident ghost.

I pressed harder. I felt no change, but an ache bloomed behind my eyes. Dammit.

"Within five feet of the fridge," I said, opening my eyes.

Florentina sat back in her chair beside me, her wide skirts ballooning around her like a layered cake. The bangles clinked together as she crossed her arms. "It's not enough."

I rubbed my forehead. "Tell me about it."

A cool hand touched my shoulder. Sympathy from the woman who we'd wrangled into this practice session.

"You are a Potesta," Florentina said, slowly, as though working through a complex calculation. "Many who came before you had to begin their training as adults. It's certainly possible. But for some reason, you aren't learning as quickly as I expected."

"Great," I said. "I'm defective."

"You're not defective," my aunt snapped. Struck a nerve with that one somehow. Interesting. Or maybe endearing. I couldn't decide. Not with my head pounding like a hollow drum.

"Maybe pick this up another time," I said. "I have class early in the morning and my head is killing me."

Florentina made a grumbling sound, but I ignored her.

A metallic whine sounded from my front hall. Mail's here. An odd moan drifted to us from the living room. Something for Marie. Often, she couldn't make noises audible to most. She hadn't been dead long enough, somehow wasn't powerful enough, to interact that fully with the world. But intense emotion could bring her partly onto this plane.

I rose from the table and took a left out of the kitchen. My feet sank into the plush blue runner that lined the hallway. It had been a gift from Tante Flora when I first moved in. The feel of it beneath me was as familiar as the creak on the stairs.

I picked up the letters below the mail slot and rifled through them. One stood out; the handwritten address looked the same as it always had. The same as the first letter that arrived a month after I moved into this old house. A few years since Marie had died upstairs.

I sliced the envelope open and set the letter on an end table in the living room.

Florentina raised an eyebrow at me as I returned to the kitchen table. "Your ghost gets mail?"

"She isn't my ghost," I said. "And it's her business, not mine."

"You're not at all curious about the letters?"

"Sure," I said. "But I like *my* privacy. Even in death, I imagine."

I washed the teacups and saucers in the sink, setting them upside down in the strainer as I went.

"Do you think whoever writes her knows she's dead?" Florentina mused.

I shrugged. "Not my business."

"It may be one day," Florentina said. I hated when her voice got deep and serious like that. Like she was telling truths that were yet to be. "Mark my words. If you and Marie run into trouble, you read those letters."

I nodded, an unfamiliar tightness settling in my chest. I didn't like the way that *if* sounded so much like *when*.

Chapter Eleven

Brigitte and I left the Academy together. Classes were still in session, but we were done for the day. The perfect chance to catch some lunch together.

We walked past the main gardens, the fountain in the middle of the path, evaporating in the midday heat. I don't know why they kept the water running It was expensive, but I supposed the parents of these students owned over half the city collectively. They could afford a few hundred gallons of water loss.

At the entrance to the school grounds was a wrought-iron gate. Images of saints welded onto it, a burnished halo of some kind around their heads. A leftover ornamental piece from a bygone era when people still believed in praying to a higher power. Back when trusting in something bigger than yourself could protect you from evil. Creatures from even the darkest folklore breaking into the human world put a damper on that kind of faith.

As Brigitte and I approached the front gates we could see the commotion just outside of them. A dozen or so parents and students had assembled. School uniforms mixed with plain clothes. A chant of some kind rose from their group, reaching past us toward the buildings at our back. Toward the Dean's office.

Teach our kids. Teach our kids.

Brigitte turned to me, her hazel eyes shining in the noonday sun. "I told you," she said. "I told you this was going to happen. The parents are involved. Things *have* to change now."

"I don't know," I said. "Look."

Brigitte turned and we both watched as Secretary Logan came down from the main school building. She wore a forest green cardigan over her white collared shirt. Brown faux leather pants tucked into soft tan boots. *Autumn chic,* I thought. She skirted the fountain and stopped directly in front of the protesters.

"You can't assemble here," she said.

"Our kids have the right to be taught," one of the parents spoke up.

I didn't point out that there was no right to that in this city. Most of the non-human citizens were left to their own devices. They either taught their own children or threw them in a public school where moments of order were so few and far between that hardly any teaching could actually occur. It was a wonder Brigitte and I had made it out of that kind of institution alive.

"Assemble if you must," Logan said. She smoothed her cardigan down her flat stomach and straightened her spine. "But you must do it over there."

I looked toward where she pointed.

The fountain?

How did that make any sense? They couldn't assemble on the sidewalk in front of the school but on school grounds was fine?

Some of the parents exchanged confused glances. I didn't blame them. One particularly bold parent with a sign that read *We Are Human* took a step forward through the school gates. A small boy followed, an unruly mop of brown hair atop his head, eyes that flashed gold in the sunlight. A shifter.

Secretary Logan gave the pair an encouraging smile and ushered the others forward with a waving hand.

"They're going to be much more obvious in the middle of the school courtyard," I said.

A grim look came on Secretary Logan's face. Her mouth fixed in a tight line. "I'm counting on it."

I tried not to stare too obviously as I looked her over. I hadn't scented anything non-human about her in our brief interactions. She sympathized with the parents, though. Why?

My nose was just beginning to itch from the proximity to her cat hair covered cardigan when she turned and strode back up the gravel walk.

Brigitte and I stood still watching the small group of parents reassemble and begin chanting again before we turned and walked onto the main avenue.

"Where did you want to go?" Brigitte asked me.

I shrugged. "Anywhere is fine."

"There's a new café off of Paulgar," she said. "Durham's. I've been meaning to try it."

"I could do a café." My phone buzzed in my back pocket, and I pulled it out.

"Meranda Haley," I said into the receiver.

"It's Nathaniel," the voice on the other end said, as though I wouldn't recognize that smiling tone he used with me.

Alarm bells rang in my head. "Is your ghost back?"

"No," he said. "I think I've got something on your amulet."

"So, it's an amulet, then?"

"Yeah, I tracked down the crew from your ship."

"And you just asked them, and they told you?"

"Yeah, whoever you sent to check them out before just didn't do their job."

"What are we dealing with?"

"It's an arcane protective amulet. Protection against, well, basically anything. Anything magical. Worth a pretty penny for sure."

"Does the crew have it?"

"No, it was truly stolen. Doesn't sound like an especially professional job. I have an idea of how you might get it back."

"Yeah?" I gave Brigitte a look. "Shoot."

"First, I have to tell you," he said. "This thing is nasty. Hard to transport. It's extremely volatile until it's assigned to someone to protect."

"Any advice on how to transport it?"

"You can take me with you," he said.

"Not a chance."

"Think about it, Meranda." He said my name with a cajoling purr. "I have the knowledge of how to move the amulet safely; I know these kinds of people; I can help with the exchange. It's the smartest move."

I clenched my jaw. I hated to bring someone along with me to a place that might get dangerous. Especially one who spent every other sentence flirting with me. It was beyond distracting.

"I can't be responsible for your safety."

"I'm not worried."

From the self-assured sound of his voice, he really wasn't.

"Okay, how do we find it?"

"Put an ad out on the amulet," he said. "Something with that much heat attached to it, I'm sure they'll be looking to get rid of it as soon as possible."

"How do I make sure they see the ad?" I shrugged my satchel further up my shoulder. "I'm not taking out space in the local paper for something like this."

"You have a computer," Nathaniel said. "I'll meet you at the Agency."

"No, not the Agency," I threw Brigitte an apologetic look. "Durham's Cafe, off Paulger Street, we're heading there now."

Brigitte shrugged. She was impossibly kind to let me interrupt our lunch.

A note of suspicion touched the voice on the other end of the phone. "We?"

"Yes, we," I said. "You're interrupting a lunch date."

I don't know what I expected. Maybe that he would assume it was a real date. That he would show some sign of jealousy at my words. What I didn't expect was what he said next:

"I'll see you and Brigitte soon."

How the hell did he know her name?

Brigitte ordered a toasted panini-like sandwich with tomatoes and mozzarella. Whatever it was, it smelled delicious. The waiter gave me a strange look when I ordered the burger off the menu. I guess in the midst of all of the fancy sandwiches and soups they didn't get very many orders for the ground beef.

I swallowed the french fries that I had in my mouth as Nathaniel walked in, nearly choking as they swallowed sideways. The sun behind him as he strode through the door put a halo around his body like the saints on the front gates of the Academy.

"That was fast," I said.

Nathaniel held his arms out at his side in a sort of shrug. "I wasn't far."

He wore a loose cotton shirt, a low V neckline on it. It showed off the sun-kissed skin of his chest. It seemed like no matter how often I saw him, that stubble on his face was the same length. I wondered if he trimmed it that way.

I scooted my metal-backed chair over to give him room to pull another seat up to the table. Brigitte raised a hand in greeting. She watched him with a clinical thoroughness, large hazel eyes taking in his whole figure. As Nathaniel turned to grab a chair, she raised her eyebrows at me. I recognized that look. She thought he was cute.

I shook my head at her.

"The safety amulet is hard to transport," Nathaniel said, sitting down. "Almost impossible if you don't know what you're doing. I'm sure they'll want to offload it here in the city."

I pulled out the laptop I had carried with me in my messenger bag and scooted my plate over so I could fit it on the table. I opened the top and typed in the password.

Nathaniel gave me a web address. Something I hadn't heard of before. It must be a site that only the less than clean businesses in the city used. I raised my eyebrows as the screen populated with pictures and advertisements for all kinds of depraved actions and items. Nathaniel gave me a slight shrug when I looked at him. Brigitte seemed to find her sandwich incredibly fascinating for the moment.

I clicked on the button to post my own ad and a blank text box populated the screen. I turned the laptop toward Nathaniel and looked over his shoulder as he typed, immediately glad I'd given him the laptop. Half the phrases he used to describe the amulet I wouldn't have come up with on my own.

"How much do you want to offer?" Nathaniel asked.

"How much do you think is right?"

Nathaniel looked to consider for a moment. "Three hundred."

"Three hundred dollars seems a little low for something that you say is this valuable."

Nathaniel leaned back in his chair and gave me a wry grin. "Three hundred *thousand*."

Brigitte choked beside me. I tried to keep my face blank. Three hundred thousand was more money than I'd see in five years. But if that's what it was worth, I was sure Mr. Poincare would pay it.

"Three hundred thousand it is," I breathed.

Nathaniel finished typing up the ad and turned the laptop back to me.

"Is that it?"

"That's it," he said.

I hit the submit button at the end of the text box.

"Now we wait," Nathaniel said. He leaned back in his chair and folded his arms behind his head. I tried to ignore the way his biceps flexed at the motion.

"Here?" I asked. "We just wait here?"

Nathaniel leaned his head back and closed his eyes. "It shouldn't take long."

I raised an eyebrow at Brigitte. She shrugged and sipped her lemonade.

A ping sounded from my laptop.

That certainly wasn't long at all.

I read the message: "315 Thou."

It was sent by a username of Anon-y-mouse. The profile picture was a half-naked cartoon female mouse with much larger breasts than a real mouse had any business possessing. I nearly rolled my eyes. Super professional group we were talking to.

Nathaniel remained still in his chair, his eyes lidded. "What does it say?" he asked. His voice was deep and quiet, almost a whisper.

"They're haggling," I said. "They want another fifteen thousand."

Half of Nathaniel's mouth quirked up. "Got 'em."

His chair legs hit the floor and he leaned his elbows on the table. The movement was so abrupt, Brigitte jumped beside me.

"Tell them that you have to talk to your employer, that you're not authorized to offer that much," he said. His blue eyes gleamed.

"Why," I asked. "I'm sure Poincare will throw in another fifteen if he needs to."

"They want to know if you're a cop," Nathaniel said. "If they push you and you accept too quickly, they'll know it's a trap."

Couldn't argue with that logic. I typed in the reply.

Immediately the answer populated the screen: "Three ten. Final offer".

Nathaniel leaned in close to read it, his heat radiating onto my arm. He nodded.

"Done," I typed.

I held my breath as the 'Anon-y-mouse is typing' indicator lit up the screen.

An address flashed on the screen, and I copied it before it could disappear.

It was replaced with: "Saturday, 9pm".

The text box disappeared.

I sat back and let out a breath. Two days wasn't long to get that much money together. I hoped Poincare would have it on hand.

"See you Saturday," Nathaniel said, pushing off from his chair.

"Nuh-uh," I said. "You're not coming."

"Don't be ridiculous," he said, turning to walk away. "Of course, I'm coming."

He didn't give me another chance to argue before he was halfway to the exit. I glared at his back.

Brigitte made a slight choking noise beside that sounded far too close to a smothered laugh. I fixed my glare on her. "Don't you start."

"He's cute," she said.

"He's not cute," I lied. "He's infuriating, and frustrating, and—"

"And cute," Brigitte said.

"Shut up," I said. I slammed the lid to my laptop shut and slid it back into the satchel. "How does he even know so much about this stuff?" I folded my arms. "Did he go to university; get a degree in some archaic subject?"

Brigitte let out a light laugh beside me. It tinkled comfortably through the air, familiar, safe.

"You can't be serious," she said.

"What do you mean?"

Brigitte gaped at me. "He's a pirate, Meranda."

What the hell?

"You didn't notice?" Brigitte asked. I was getting awfully perturbed by the way her hazel eyes danced with laughter at my expense. "I mean just look at him. With a swagger like that he has to be a pirate. That's how he knows so much about banned items in this city. He's smuggled them for a living."

"That's ridiculous," I said.

"No, it's hilarious," Brigitte said. Her voice dropped low so only I could hear. "You're a mermaid; he's a pirate. It's the oldest story ever told."

"Not a chance," I said.

Brigitte laughed again. "You mark my words. You two are star-crossed. For good or ill; it's in your nature."

I wasn't sure I liked the sound of that.

Chapter Twelve

The lobby of Janus Poincare's business practically screamed luxury. No uncomfortable plush chairs which may have an indeterminable stain on the seat. No, for Poincare's clients only the solid black leather couches would do. The double door and floor-to-ceiling windows that made up the front of the building allowed for a cheery brightness when the sunlight streamed in, only slightly muted by the frosted glass.

Poincare's company name and a logo of laurel wreaths were painted in black on the windows on either side of the front doors. Strictly symmetrical. The tile floor was a white marble so shiny and clean it looked as though there was a sheen of glass over top. Not a scuff mark in sight. My footsteps echoed as I walked across the lobby to the greeting desk.

"May I help you?" The woman behind the desk flashed me a brilliant smile. She wore a ruffled white and black polka-dotted blouse. A headset crossed over the curly hair, but not a ringlet moved out of place. Earrings hung from her earlobes, three chains of silver dangling nearly to the top of each shoulder. Her name was set into a silver rectangle pinned to her blouse over her heart. Peggy.

The chair she sat on behind the desk, kept Peggy at eye level. The desk itself was a monolith of shiny black marble. I was dwarfed before it, inadequate somehow despite the efforts I'd made to fit into Poincare's world. I wore my nicest black slacks and white blouse. A suit jacket that matched the slacks and ruffled along the small of my back, hung from my shoulders unbuttoned.

"Meranda Haley," I said. I made to lean against the surface of the desk and thought better of it. I wouldn't like to be responsible for smudging fingerprints onto the surface. "I have an appointment with Mr. Poincare."

"Of course, Ms. Haley," Peggy said. "I'll let him know you're here. Take a seat."

I thanked her and turned toward the square of couches. In the midst of them was a low table. Its legs were black rods, industrial, like the railing of the staircase across the room. The surface was the same frosted glass as the front windows.

I took a seat on the couch nearest the door. The cushion was harder than I expected, all support and no sink. I ran a hand along the smooth leather surface. Not even a fleck of lint. I had a feeling Oleksandr would like this place.

I looked up at the tap, tap, tap of heels on the polished floor.

"Mr. Poincare is ready for you," Peggy said as she approached. "Come with me please."

I fell into step beside her and tried not to stare at the height of the heels she wore. They were black, same as mine, but they looked infinitely more expensive. The material had a matte finish to it that matched the pencil-style skirt she wore. She led me to the stairs. Her small hands were clasped before her, and she walked as though she were floating. I gripped the handrail as my unfamiliar heels put me off balance. Dammit. If only I could wear combat boots to business meetings, I'd be unstoppable.

A hallway stretched before us when we reached the top of the stairs. Peggy paused and checked behind her once to be sure I was following before she started down the hallway. I wondered absentmindedly who covered the desk for her while she was taking me to Poincare. The glass enclosed conference rooms we passed were completely empty. Maybe Poincare was the only one in the building. Certainly, he wouldn't have booked another appointment too close to mine. The lobby was probably safe.

Peggy stopped before the last door on the left and rapped twice with her knuckles before returning to her previous position. Her hands remained clasped before her, just over her diaphragm. Her back was straight as though she was at attention, feet planted firmly in those impossible heels.

I straightened beside her, aware then that there was a scuff on my left shoe. How the hell had that happened? It wasn't there when I left this morning.

"Come in," the deep voice called from behind the door.

Peggy gave me another brilliant smile. I returned it before realizing that she was just fixing it onto her face for her employer. She pushed open the door and swung her arms wide.

"Ms. Haley is here for you-u-u," she drew out the last syllable in a sing-song voice that nearly made me cringe and ended with a flourish and a small bow.

Janus Poincare rose from behind his desk. I had envisioned something more. At the sight of the lobby, I had pictured ornate solid wood desks and dark high-backed furniture. An expensive suit and an overwhelming scent of cologne.

Instead, a thin plank of black wood made up the desk surface, held up by thin metal bars. The room was smaller than I expected, a lone couch against the one wall that wasn't completely taken up by floor to ceiling windows. A beverage cart with glass shelves stood beside the couch. And the man behind the desk, was as understated as his office.

He wore black slacks and a white, fitted button up. Shiny shoes peeked at me from behind the metal bars of his desk, glinting in the daylight that streamed in through the windows. His face was clean shaven and kind crinkles lit beside his eyes. He had to be around Dad's age, and his well-combed hair was just beginning to show a peppering of silver at his temples.

"Miss Haley, welcome," Poincare said. He gestured to the couch. "Please, have a seat."

He waved Peggy out of the room with more words of gratitude than I expected from someone with such wealth and power. He was almost gentle with her. Peggy flashed him another smile before she left, closing the door behind her. I understood why she'd want to impress him.

I took my seat. The couch was much softer than the ones downstairs. I wondered for a second if he sometimes slept on its surface, the way I had fallen asleep on Dad's beat up, green couch after a late night of work.

Poincare leaned a hip on the side of his desk and crossed his arms. "So, I hear you've found it."

My mouth went dry. I tried to not to let the nerves get to me. Not when I forced my feet into these low heels that pinched my toes, not when I walked across that echoing lobby. But here, with my client staring me down, knowing that my father would have rather bankrupted the business than sit in this office across from him. I found myself grasping for words.

"You worked faster than I expected," he said. He didn't seem to notice my discomfort, or perhaps he chose to ignore it.

I cleared my throat. "We're a small team, but we work well together."

Poincare raised a single dark eyebrow. "Very well," he said. "So where is it?"

He sounded as though he'd expected me to bring it with me. I hadn't had a chance to get him on the phone, needing to arrange this meeting with his secretary. There wasn't time to give her the details of what I needed.

"I don't have it," I said. "Yet," I amended as Poincare made to push off the desk.

"Why are you here?" he asked. His voice was calm and measured. Even as a placid lake. I wondered what roiled beneath.

"We found the individuals who have your property," I said, choosing my words with all the tact Dad had taught me. "We've set up an exchange for it. When we originally spoke about your case, you said you'd be willing to pay a reward for its return."

Poincare walked to the beverage cart and turned over one of the glass tumblers that sat on its top. "So, you've orchestrated an exchange," he said.

I nodded, then realized he wasn't looking at me. "Yes, this weekend."

My client poured himself a glass of amber liquid. The strangely sweet burn of whiskey tickled my nostrils. To my surprise he held the glass out to me.

"I'm on the clock," I said, hoping he'd take the clue without me having to outright reject his offer.

"Surely, you can have just one," he said.

I watched the amber liquid turn in the glass, the sunlight shining through it casting rainbows across the wall. It would be a simple thing, taking the glass. I had practiced keeping the static at bay even after consuming a light drink or two, but that much? That strong a drink? I thought of Nathaniel and his haunting. If I received a call from him and I couldn't help, I would never forgive myself.

"Mr. Poincare, I treat every case for every client with the utmost seriousness and sobriety. With all due respect, you are not my only client. I must decline."

A glint of something close to respect lit in Poincare's dark eyes. He nodded once and sat on the arm of the couch, rotating the glass under his own nose. He inhaled the burning scent before taking a small sip. His eyes closed as he swallowed, as though the mere feeling of it was ecstasy.

I was tempted to look away from the display.

"How much?" Poincare asked at last.

"What?"

"How much do they want?"

"Three hundred and ten thousand dollars."

Poincare took another sip; his eyes narrowed in calculation.

"Done," he said, standing so quickly I nearly startled. "Peggy will have the money for you downstairs."

"Thank you," I said. "You'll have your property in hand by Monday."

"I'll take that on your word." He nodded toward the door, and I took that as my clue to leave.

My last sight of him was with the phone receiver against his cheek, calling down to Peggy to prepare the money.

Before I left the building, I had three hundred ten thousand dollars in an unmarked black duffel.

It was heavier than I expected.

Samuel was back at the Agency when I returned. He sat behind my dad's desk, fiddling with the computer mouse.

"Any progress on getting the web access back?" I asked.

Samuel shook his head, still focused on the screen.

I dropped the duffel bag onto the couch with a definite thud. Samuel looked up.

"What's that?"

"Three hundred ten thousand dollars," I said as nonchalantly as I could manage.

Samuel blinked once.

I examined one fingernail, waiting for him to ask me where I'd gotten it, or what it was for, or *something*.

Samuel's face remained frozen. His jaw slackened.

"Do you have a reset button I need to push or something?" I asked.

"Mer," Samuel said slowly, "I know we need the money, but—"

I straightened.

"Did you *steal* that?"

"What?" I said, louder than I meant to. "No, of course not!"

Samuel came around the desk, he held his hand out before him as though I might be a wounded animal who would attack at the slightest provocation.

"I didn't steal it," I said, laughing to put him at ease. "It's a ransom for the amulet that Poincare lost."

Samuel dropped his arm. "Well why didn't you say that when you walked in? And what ransom? It's an amulet? Why haven't I heard about any of this?"

"I tried to call you," I pointed out. "More than once the last few days. You didn't pick up."

"I'm sorry if I was busy trying to track down some leads," Samuel said. He crossed his arms. I tried not to stare at the muscles in his forearms, flexing in his anger. "I didn't have a chance to answer my phone."

"Did you find anything?"

A muscle twitched in his cheek. "No," he said. "I still have a few leads to follow up on."

"Well, while you were unreachable," I said, turning to the duffel, "I got the name of the ship that was carrying Poincare's missing cargo, found the crew, found what was missing, and coordinated a buy for it." I paused and waited for the cries of adulation.

"You didn't do all that on your own," Samuel pointed out.

"Well, no," I said, resisting the urge to defend my honor. "Oleksandr helped—"

"Oh, that's perfect," Samuel said, turning away. "The bloodsucker is around the *one* time I'm not and you go running off with him."

"Running off with—" I shook my head. "What are you talking about? You weren't there to talk to and I'm not looking for your *permission* anyway. Why the hell are we even fighting about this?"

I held up a hand before he could respond. I didn't want to yell. "I asked Oleksandr for help and he gave it. He came through. Without him, I wouldn't have found the name of the ship. Without his contact, I wouldn't have any of this information."

"Great, now you're trusting a contact that Oleksandr introduced? He's a *vampire*, Mer," Samuel's voice rose. I resisted the urge to cringe. He'd never raised his voice at me before.

"Why are you so hateful against anyone in this city who doesn't act like you?" I demanded. "First you spend weeks drilling me on the weight of a silver bullet, because of course *any shifter* could turn on me and attack, and I better know how to defend myself. Now, you're going to argue against a lead that could solve this entire case just because it came from Oleksandr? Come on, Sammy."

I didn't tell him that I had in fact been attacked by a trio of werewolves the day before and he was damn right about me needing to know how to defend myself against them. I was too angry to concede that point.

"Maybe we should have never taken this case," Samuel said. "Maybe Poincare is a lying thieving con artist who just wants you to fail so he can hold it over your head for the rest of this Agency's existence."

I let his last words hang in the air. It was what I worried about before Nathaniel finally found our amulet. I hated that he'd voiced that out loud.

"Enough," I said. "I don't care what you have against Oleksandr. Honestly, right now, I don't care what's going on in your life to make you act this way. You're being an ass and I will not stand for it in my dad's own office."

Samuel clenched his jaw. I watched the muscles in his cheek work, pulling his dark skin taut. Damn it. I didn't want to fight. But my cheeks burned, and my eyes stung from the words we'd exchanged.

"Get out," I said finally. "I need a night. You can come back tomorrow. We leave at eight thirty for the exchange. If you're not here, I'm leaving without you."

"Fine," Samuel said.

I stood still as he stepped around me to pluck his jacket

off the back of the couch. I don't know what I wanted him to say. Maybe I wanted him to apologize, to beg me to not send him away. I certainly didn't expect the next words out of his mouth.

"Your agency is never going to make it if you keep calling this your dad's office. Take it seriously, Mer. There's more on the line than just getting the internet back."

He left before I could respond.

Chapter Thirteen

The water was warm against my scales. It wasn't always nice this far into October, but it had been an unusually warm day. I stretched my arms in the current, expanding my ribs and allowing my gills to open wide. Cypress trees emerged from the water here and there. Their trunks solid obstacles to my swim, roots spreading deep into the swamp floor. Thirsty.

It wasn't every day that I dove into the bayou. But today, with so much on my mind, it seemed impossible not to. Maybe the words Samuel and I had spoken would wash off in the water. If I closed my eyes, I could imagine that our fight had been a dream. Something cold passed beneath me, a familiar shudder in the water.

Spirits lived in these swamps. Those who had lost their lives to fickle environmental disasters or fickle human disasters alike, were left to haunt these waters. I could feel their presence. For the most part, they rested fitfully beneath the surface. My shields were up. They wouldn't bother me today.

My tail moved powerfully beneath me. The fin spread wide like a blue curtain. It was absolute freedom stretching it through the water. This particular bayou was a favorite of mine. Brackish water forming where the salt from the Gulf met the runoff from rivers and springs. I didn't dare enter the Gulf itself, not when I could be sensed by any melusine nearby. But here, this saltiness did my scales good.

I flicked my tail lazily above the surface of the water, watching it. Watching how the sunlight reflected sparkles off it. Metallic shades of blue and green glittered in the rays.

"I thought I'd find you here."

I pulled my tail beneath the surface and sank down until only my head was above the water. I'd been seen. I rotated slowly toward the shore, ready to dive beneath the surface and swim miles upstream. Leaving my clothes behind would be a hassle, but I'd get them back.

I let out a breath as I saw who had spoken, bubbles exploding from my gills.

"You could've scared me to death," I said. "You can't just sneak up on someone like that."

Brigitte laughed her light tinkling laugh. "You should have been paying more attention," she said.

I made as though to splash water her direction, but she stopped me with a raised hand.

"Don't you dare get my hair wet," Brigitte said. "I just got it done, and it's perfect."

I wanted very badly to splash her anyway. But I wouldn't be blamed for her hair being ruined on its first day.

I floated closer to the bank of the swamp to make talking easier.

"Did you need something?"

Brigitte lowered herself down on the bank sitting cross

legged, her dark blue skinny jeans were tucked into brown leather boots. The fashionable kind that rose midway up her calf. Not the functional kind like I would've chosen. She pulled the sleeves of her white sweater up her brown fore-arms and leaned her chin on one hand.

"I need to ask a favor," she said.

"Whatever you need," I said. I flicked my tail back-and-forth, the length of it beating against the water, holding me in place so I didn't drift away as she spoke.

"I need to use your dad's lab," Brigitte said.

Consider my curiosity piqued. Other than for cases, I had hardly ever seen my dad use his lab. And when he used it, I was hardly ever allowed in it.

I suppose he never forgave me for the one beaker I knocked over in middle school that contained liquid which promptly ate through his workbench. I think he would have, had I not told him how silly I thought he looked running to fetch a powder which would neutralize the acid before it started eating through the floor tiles too. I had been banned ever since.

"One condition," I said.

"Yes?"

I gave her a smile. "You let me watch."

My hair still hung damp on my shoulders when we made it back to the Agency. I wore the black T-shirt and light blue jeans that I had left on the bank before my swim. Brigitte generously turned around while I dressed. It wasn't like she hadn't seen all of me before.

I used my key to open the door to Dad's office, and

dropped my satchel on the couch as we walked in. It was only a short walk from my favorite swimming spot. Brigitte had spent none of it telling me what she needed Dad's lab for. I wasn't sure if that meant it was important and confidential and she didn't want anyone else to hear on the way. Or if it just meant her work was completely unimportant, and I shouldn't be so interested in it. Either way, her silence only served to make me more curious. That, and the black tote bag she had slung over one shoulder.

A second key from the ring that Dad had left for me opened the laboratory at the back of his office. I always liked how unassuming the door was. It nearly blended into the wall in which it stood. From the couch in Dad's office, one would never know that it was there, partially blocked by a coat rack. That was the way Dad liked it.

The door open, Brigitte took a deep breath beside me. To me it smelled like chemicals and cleaning fluids, but to her I was sure it smelled like home.

I flipped the light on and blinked as fluorescent bulbs reflected off the white tile floors and shone on the dark gray workbench.

"Nothing's changed," Brigitte said.

"No one's been here to change it."

Along the wall to our right stood a glass cabinet, the shelves lined with the glass beakers and graduated cylinders. Beside it, a locked cabinet with meticulously labeled acids and bases. Everything you could need in a functioning laboratory.

Brigitte spoke as she crossed the room to the main cabinet. "The last time I was in here, your dad was working a case with a pack of werewolves."

"A pack?" I asked. Pack organization was outlawed in

the Crescent City. It had been ever since the first alphas moved in. An organized group of shifters was too dangerous for the humans. Any hint of a pack forming was stamped out with extreme prejudice these days. At this point, most alphas moved out of the city, happy to try their hand in the wilderness with a pack rather than live in the city without one.

"It turned out not to be a pack," Brigitte said. "It wasn't a shifter at all."

I pulled a stool over beside the workbench and sat on it. Brigitte opened the glass case and pulled out two beakers, a Bunsen burner, and a couple stands I didn't know the names of.

"We had saliva," she continued. "DNA left over from crime scenes. We thought if we could prove that it was shifters, and more than one, we'd have evidence of a pack forming."

"Was this a private client?"

Brigitte dropped her load on the workbench, keeping the beakers apart so they wouldn't clack against one another. "Police Department consult," she said. "They just needed evidence, and they were going to be raiding the slums; clearing out the streets west of Bourbon."

I stifled a shudder. That kind of mass purge hadn't taken place in nearly a decade. I barely remembered the last one. Except for the parts I couldn't forget.

"I'm sure Dad was glad when the results came back; not a shifter," I murmured.

"Indeed he was," Brigitte said. She set up her equipment, lighting the Bunsen with her flint. She set her tote bag gently on the workbench. The black bag was one I had bought for her in high school. She'd complained that she didn't have enough hands to carry all her books to and from the library at school, and I had needed very little prompting to gift her the most ridiculous tote I could find. The front of it, in swooping white letters said, Book Baby, a cartoon image of a book in a swaddling blanket beneath.

I thought I'd have plenty of time to tease her about it at school, but it was the following week that I was sent to the Gulf. When I'd returned, she had left for her training in Atlanta. The tote had gone with her. I couldn't believe she still had it.

Not holding books today, I noted as Brigitte pulled out a softball-sized object wrapped in white cloth. She added clear liquid to a beaker from a jar labeled with an unpronounceable name and set the beaker over the Bunsen to heat.

I tried not to ask too many questions, but my mind was practically buzzing with them. Especially when Brigitte put on gloves before she removed the wrapping to reveal an Old-Fashioned whiskey glass.

I leaned forward, unable to stop myself.

"What is it?

"It's called a tumbler, I think," Brigitte said.

I almost responded with a hearty, 'No shit, Sherlock', but paused when I saw her smile.

"You're teasing me," I said.

Brigitte didn't answer, but her hazel eyes danced.

"We're testing the DNA left on the glass," she said. She set the glass down flat and pulled out a collection swab.

"Do you need to pull prints, too? I think I remember where Dad kept his kit."

"No need," Brigitte murmured. "I know whose it is."

My mind practically screamed. It wasn't usually this difficult to get information out of her. The liquid above the burner began to bubble and Brigitte turned the burner off.

She donned thick gloves and a set of goggles and poured a white powder into the beaker. She waved me back before swirling the concoction. I raised an eyebrow as the clear liquid bloomed to a bright purple.

"What's that for?"

"It detects the Lycan virus," Brigitte said. "Causes it to glow under certain lights."

"Cool."

She smeared the cotton swab on a plate of agar and poured the purple liquid over the top, forming a shallow layer over the substrate. The plate went into a black box that stood on a counter on the other side of the room. With a shiny dark outside and single glass window, it looked like nothing so much as a cheap microwave.

"Now we wait," she said.

Ah, yes. My strong suit.

"How long?"

"A few days," Brigitte said, putting the supplies away.

I was itching for answers already. It made me want to crawl out of my skin, this not knowing.

"I could never be a chemist."

Brigitte let out a chuckle. "No, you probably couldn't."

It was nearly noon. Still nine hours to go until the exchange.

"Lunch?"

"Absolutely."

I returned to the Agency around seven in the evening. There were a few things I wanted to make sure were in place before we left for the exchange. Florentina's parlour was empty. I wasn't sure when her last reading was, but she'd turned the lights out before she left. I flicked the hall light on.

I checked the duffel I had locked up in the coat closet in Dad's office. I would have kept it by my side, but it made me antsy carrying that much around with me. A part of me was sure that the money inside was going to disappear.

It was still there.

I refreshed the Internet one time on the desktop computer. It was a habit I'd picked up that I hoped I wouldn't have to use much longer. The computer remained unfazed by my efforts.

Sammy walked in around eight o'clock. He barely said hi to me but sat on the couch and pulled out his phone.

I tried to ignore the tense silence he brought with him. I fiddled with the fake plant behind the keyboard on Dad's desk and watched him out of the corner of my eye.

A part of me wanted us to talk it out. I didn't want to be fighting. But I knew there was a good chance if we started hashing it out now, we would just get more pissed at each other, and I couldn't bring that kind of distraction with me to the exchange tonight.

I was glad he'd shown up, though. Even when we were fighting, I still trusted him to watch my back before anyone else.

A knock on the front door told me that Nathaniel had arrived. Samuel gave me a strange look as I passed him on the couch to answer the door. In all our fighting yesterday, I hadn't told him that Nathaniel was coming.

Dammit.

Nathaniel walked into Dad's office with a swagger that I only noticed because Brigitte had pointed it out the day before. A pirate. I was never going to look at him the same again.

Samuel rose from the couch as we walked in. "Who's that?" he asked.

"This is Nathaniel," I said. "Nathaniel, this is Samuel."

The two of them regarded one another with the kind of calculation that I expected stray dogs to use when trying to determine which one of them was alpha.

"Nathaniel is our artifacts expert," I said. I walked past the two of them to Dad's desk to pick up the duffel bag. "He's coming with us to the exchange."

Samuel seemed to decide that now was the time to put his foot down. "It's a bad idea," he said. "I don't know him. I don't like it."

"Sammy," I said. "Don't make this a thing. He's the one who found us our crew. He's the one who found the amulet. He comes because he can verify what it is we are looking for."

Nathaniel seemed to be doing his best impression of an innocent doe. He widened his eyes and held his arms out at his side as though to show he was unarmed. I didn't believe it for one second. There was no way he was walking in here without a weapon of some kind.

Samuel didn't seem to buy it either. "You should've told me, Mer," he said.

"To be fair," Nathaniel said. "She didn't tell me you were coming either."

I turned on him. "That's because I don't owe you shit."

I looked at Samuel hoping he could see the apology in my eyes.

"I don't like it," Samuel repeated. "I think we should reschedule the exchange."

I rubbed a hand on my forehead. "We can't do that. It's all set, and I promised Poincare he'd have his amulet by Monday."

Samuel's jaw worked for a few seconds before he spoke. "You owe me better than this, Meranda," he said. "First, you don't give me the courtesy of updating me this entire investigation. Now, you bring someone else into it without even an attempt to let me know. I won't be pressured into going into a warehouse without knowing all the facts. Not again."

I opened my mouth to say something. To apologize, or, I don't know, something. But Samuel held up a hand. "No, don't." His lips were almost white as they pressed against each other. "I'm out."

Something in my chest fluttered. Almost a panic. I took a quick breath. "You can't just be out."

"Tough shit," he said. "I'm out. If you don't trust me enough to keep me in the loop, I don't want any part of it."

The something in my chest hardened. It wasn't panic anymore. It was anger.

"This exchange happens with or without you," I said. "It's not my timeline we're operating under."

"Then go," Samuel said. "You seem to be doing everything else on your own. Go to the exchange too."

"She won't be on her own," Nathaniel said. "I'll be there." He looked to be about as pleased as any cat who found a canary unawares.

Samuel took one look at Nathaniel and left. The door to the Agency slammed behind him, the little bell above it jingling cheerfully.

Damn bell.

Less than ten minutes later, Nathaniel and I were on a streetcar heading in the direction of the warehouse district. I kept the duffel on my lap. I didn't want just anyone knowing what was inside of it. With the number of inter-esting characters who rode public transportation in this city, no one was going to pay attention to a couple of humans with a bag.

Nathaniel allowed me silence. I think he knew how badly I'd wanted Samuel to be with us. But his shoulder jostled against mine with each bump on the road, a reminder that he was still there.

Even with Samuel gone, I would have done the exchange on my own if I had to, but it was good to have someone with me. I couldn't explain why but there was something familiar about Nathaniel. About the scent that came off him. I knew it was a trick my mind was playing on me. I knew it was just because he smelled like home, all salt and sun and water. Or maybe it was just Brigitte's words, 'you're star-crossed, for good or ill'. I snuck a glance at the man beside me. He smiled at a pair of shy pixie kids across the car. I supposed there could be worse people on my team.

We got off on Camp Street. Two other passengers in worker's uniforms got off at the same stop. Nathaniel and I waited until they passed on their way, joking back-and-forth about how much they'd rather be drinking than working. Once they were out of sight, we turned in the direction of the address we were looking for.

The Warehouse District had gone through a number of rebrandings. Old rectangular buildings that once held mills or copper manufacturing, spent some time as restaurants and smoothie shops before the portals opened. This place was hit hard in the chaos that followed. Nathaniel and I passed a brick structure that was half demolished. Jagged edges of red bricks and exposed re-bar stuck out into the walkway. We skirted around it.

Graffiti brought color to the neighborhood. Greens and reds stood stark against the gray and white buildings. A slogan of a local shifter gang caught my eye. A gray wolf snarling from within a red shield. If Samuel was with us, he'd be checking for the weight of his pistol, I knew. I pushed the thought away.

We didn't walk for long before Nathaniel pointed ahead. I tracked his hand. Our address was a two-story white brick structure. It seemed to have survived the portals opening unscathed. Windows were set high on the second floor, no fire escape leading down from them. No exit there unless you could fly. The first floor appeared solid save for the door facing us.

The building didn't look particularly inviting.

"Do we knock?" I asked.

Nathaniel shrugged. "What are they going to do, shoot us? They don't know we have their money yet." He pushed the door open with a creak that I was certain alerted the entire warehouse to our arrival.

I didn't bother pointing out that they could in fact shoot us and check in our duffel after if there was money in it or not. Nathaniel passed through the threshold. No turning back now.

I followed him through the door.

As soon as we'd ducked into the building, I drew up short. Directly in front of us was a unit of metal shelves. Their sides were lined with a plastic sheet that snapped like the sails of a ship from the breeze we brought in with us. I was sure anyone inside would've heard us by now, but still I paused, listening. No one called out or shot at us. That was a good sign.

The only way to go was forward so we pressed on. As we moved around the shelves, the floor opened before us. Our steps echoed through the bare room. Aside from the shelves that offered a buffer between the main room and the door, nothing occupied the structure save for a long table and the two men standing behind it.

On the table was a small metal case, hardly bigger than a toaster. I was sure what we came to purchase was inside of it.

As we stepped forward one of the men spoke. "Did you bring the money?"

I almost held up the duffel bag I had slung over my shoulder and then thought better of it. "Do you have our amulet?" I called out.

The man on the left gestured to the case on the table. I took the opportunity to look him over. He wore jeans and a black t-shirt that I was certain was two sizes larger than he needed. The perfect cover for a weapon tucked into a waistband. His skin was pockmarked, and greasy strands of brown hair hung limp on his forehead. His mouth was formed into what looked to be a permanent frown.

The partner appeared younger, maybe mid-thirties, bald with a scraggly brown beard and teeth that shone yellow as he spoke. "See for yourself," he said.

I motioned Nathaniel forward, giving him a chance to look at the case and hung back with the duffel. I couldn't tell for sure from where I was standing with the table between us if either man was armed, but if I were in their position, I would be. It seemed as though the entire room was holding its breath. The weight of the hot warehouse pressing in on us all. Nathaniel undid the latch on the case with a metallic snap and lifted the lid.

Nathaniel peered into the case and the man on the right shifted from one foot to the other. I watched his movement out of the corner of my eye. I hoped the nervous movement didn't mean he was planning on doing something stupid. Nervous humans liked to do things that were stupid. A sheen of sweat stood out on his brow as we all waited for Nathaniel's verdict.

"It's legit," Nathaniel said.

The bald man's shoulders sagged in visible relief. Almost as if he hadn't been sure. They had to know the amulet was real, right? Why else would we be doing all of this?

I made to step forward to place the duffel on the table, but Nathaniel held up a hand.

"We're not paying you for this," Nathaniel said.

I tried to tamp down the strangled noise that rose in my throat. He couldn't be serious.

The bearded man's face turned the shade of a ripe turnip. "What do you mean you ain't payin'?"

Nathaniel leaned his hands on the table, the picture of ease.

I was behind him, but I could hear the smile in his voice as he said, "You want to get rid of this more badly than we need it."

What? He had to be bluffing. It had to be some kind of a trick. I couldn't believe he was doing this now.

"In fact," Nathaniel continued. "You're so willing to get rid of this thing you'd probably pay *us* to take it."

I stopped my jaw before it had a chance to hit the floor. I wanted to yell at him. I wanted to tell him to cut it out before the two men in front of us pulled out guns and started shooting. But just as I opened my mouth to speak, the man on the left broke down.

"Ye-es." His voice cracked on the word. "Please take it. We didn't know what we were getting ourselves into. It's making us so sick."

"Shut up, Louie," the bearded man said.

"It's probably destroying the rest of your inventory too," Nathaniel said.

The bearded man looked as though he would hold out for a moment longer, but to my surprise he actually agreed. "We can't store it next to anything," he said. "It eats through any container we put it in. We probably have less than half an hour in the case it's in now. The thing is cursed. It's evil."

I could hardly believe what I was hearing. Exchanges didn't happen this easily. There had to be something wrong.

Nathaniel's voice was gentle when he spoke again. "We'll just be taking it off your hands then."

The bearded man stepped forward and almost put his hand on the lid but snatched his palm back at the last moment.

"Not so fast," he said. "What about our money? I think you owe us something."

Nathaniel stepped back from the table with a sort of shrug. "Or we could just leave you with it. See how much more of your profits it eats through before you find some other sucker to pawn it off on."

I held my breath. The two of them looked at each other as though considering. Then Louie made a grimace. "I don't want to take it back with us," he said.

The bearded man wrapped his sleeve around his hand and pushed the case across the table towards Nathaniel. "Take it," he said. "We're better off finding something else."

Nathaniel sat his backpack on the table and zipped it

open. He pulled out a solid looking black box. I didn't know what it was made of. If this thing could eat through metal, I couldn't think of what element would contain it. Nathaniel's box had the kind of matte exterior that you'd see on a piece of Kevlar. The two thieves seemed to watch with interest as Nathaniel took their box and put it in his own. As he pulled his hand away, I noticed his palm reddening even from the brief contact with the amulet's container. Not for the first time I was grateful he'd come along. I don't know what I would've done if that thing burned through my skin.

I would have liked if the other two men left first. Now they knew that there was a way to transport the amulet safely, there would be nothing stopping them from attacking us and taking both the transportation box and the money now.

I leveled them with my gaze. "Now," I said, pouring an ounce of my power into my voice. "We are going to leave. Why don't you two stay where you are for another five minutes. When we are good and gone, you go on your way." I kept my voice level and sweet. I wasn't controlling, I was suggesting. Powerfully hinting.

Both men nodded to my words. A glazed look entered their eyes.

I didn't fail to notice the shudder that passed through Nathaniel at my words. He tried to hide it, keeping his face neutral. But I saw it nonetheless.

I settled the duffel more comfortably on my shoulder as Nathaniel swung the backpack up. We turned and left the warehouse.

I looked back once to make sure the men weren't following us.

They weren't.

We got as far as the streetcar stop before we spoke again.

I whirled on him. "What the hell kind of stunt was that?"

Nathaniel threaded his thumbs through the straps of the backpack and gave me a tiny shrug. "It worked didn't it?"

"Sure it worked," I said. "But what were you thinking?"

"I was thinking," Nathaniel said, "that maybe you'd want to save Mr. Poincare some money. If we could get out of there, amulet in hand, without paying, why wouldn't we?"

"There's more to all of this than money," I said. "My name has to bear some kind of reliability in this city. My agency can't survive if people can't trust me. That means thieves too. Who's going to set up an exchange with Collier investigations if they can't trust that we'll give them what's agreed upon. Just because in your line of work money trumps all—"

"Money isn't all I care about," Nathaniel snapped. He turned away. His shoulders towards me for a brief instant as he looked up the street. It looked as though he was watching to see if our streetcar was approaching. I couldn't help but wonder if my words had offended him somehow, hurt him maybe.

"I didn't mean—" I started. I didn't know what to say, where to even start. "Why don't you show me how to transport this so I can get it back to Poincare safely."

"Oh, you're not taking it back to Poincare," Nathaniel said.

I can't have heard him right. "What?"

"This isn't what Poincare lost," Nathaniel said.

"You're joking."

"Not in the slightest. This is for me."

I searched his eyes for a hint of humor. It wasn't there.

"What was all this for, then?" I nearly yelled. I tried to breathe deeply, hold back the tide of anger. It was a visceral rage that crested like a wave in my chest. "Where's Poincare's amulet? What the hell is in that box?"

"I don't know where Poincare's shit is," Nathaniel said. He took a step back and I realized I was leaning toward him with what I was sure was a murderous look in my eyes.

"I needed you to put out the ad because no one in the city would deal with me."

I swallowed against the lump that was rising in my throat. My feet were frozen to the sidewalk. All I could think was that I promised Poincare. "I promised him that we would have his amulet back by Monday."

"That sounds like a you problem," Nathaniel said.

I considered for a moment taking the bag from him. Pushing him down and pulling it off his shoulders. Running up the street before he could give chase. But from his size, he was stronger than I was and despite Harnock's training I wasn't that fast.

"Why would you do this?" I asked, finally.

"It's a safety amulet," he said. "I need it to protect me from the ghosts."

"That's what I'm supposed to be doing," I hissed.

"No," he said. The word fell like lead. "I can't trust you to do that." The streetlight shone in his eyes. What was normally a calm blue now practically glowed with intense emotion.

"What do you mean you can't trust me?" I asked. "This is what you hired me to do."

"You tried to kill me!" Nathaniel yelled.

I flinched instinctively. I nearly brought my hands up in defense.

"What?"

Nathaniel took two paces away from me. Two fists touched his forehead before he punched them towards the ground. He swung back around to face me.

"You don't even *remember*?"

I shook my head. I had no earthly idea what he could mean.

He raised a finger my direction. Gone was the flirtatious man who had sat beside me at Baxter's. Gone was that dimple that pulled his mouth into a half-smirk as he teased me. The face before me, twisted with anger, I didn't even recognize.

"Twelve years ago," he said. His voice stabbed like ice crystals in my heart. "Twelve years ago, in the middle of the *fucking* ocean, you tried to kill me." He took a shaky breath. "So, forgive me if I don't put my life in your hands."

I froze.

Twelve years ago, I was training in the Gulf with the melusines.

Twelve years ago, I spent months without ever seeing a human...

Except once.

The world crashed around me. Memories I had held back, memories I had suppressed, flooded into my mind. The young face in a boat above me. The surface of the water shimmering between us. My song luring, luring.

Blood pounded in my ears. The world muffled by its thundering beat.

I closed my eyes against the memories. Against what I had tried to do.

I understood now. I understood why he acted like he

knew me. I understood why he seemed to know so much about me.

We had met before.

And I had tried to kill him.

When I opened my eyes, he was gone.

Chapter Fourteen

"Do you remember where I was twelve years ago?" Dad's voice emerged from somewhere north of the coffee table. "Somewhere between the Gulf and the Caribbean islands, I think. I didn't get many details, though."

I drew my knees up to my chest, settling my weight into the couch. "Yeah, somewhere like that."

I blinked a few times trying to clear the glassiness from my eyes. I was sure that Dad knew how little I wanted to explain what happened. He helped fill the silence.

"You never gave me the details," he said. "You don't have to tell me if you don't want to."

I squeezed my eyes shut. I really did have to tell him, though. It was time.

I could see it in my mind's eye, the warm blue of the Gulf waters. The groups of melusines, more than I'd seen together in my entire young life.

"You dropped me off with Marianna and her family," I began. "You know they live deep in the Gulf, closer to Texas than the rest of the melusines. Did you know why?"

The rush of cold wafted over me like a cool breeze. Or like a soft exhale.

"They were banished from the rest of the melusines," he said. "After they helped the humans in the war, after they stood up to General Lo'Tan, they were marked as traitors. When your abilities started manifesting, I didn't know where else to send you, but I trusted them."

"But Marianna didn't tell you that they couldn't train me," I said.

A surprised noise sounded across the room. He was drifting, his spirit unable to stay in one place as I spoke.

"They couldn't train a melusine who inherited the siren's call," I said. "Any who were born into their glamour were sent to the main pod. Lo'Tan hadn't been in power there for years. The tensions between the two groups remained, but the main pod had to take the others in for training. It's too dangerous to leave a siren untrained. Even just one left to her own devices could wreak havoc on the entire ecosystem."

The silence hung heavy for a moment like the pressure of being underwater, sinking deeper and deeper. I took a breath. "Marianna didn't explain who I was when she dropped me off with my people. As far as they knew I was one of her glamor. Just a melusine child they didn't know existed yet. One other from Marianna's family came with me, Tatiana. She was just coming of age, like me, coming into her power. The two of us, and four from the main pod all trained together."

I could see Tatiana then, drifting before my eyes as she did the day we first arrived near Bermuda. Her dark hair floating in a cloud of coils around her face. With her dark skin and obsidian tail she was almost a shadow against the ocean floor. Beautiful and dangerous.

I shook myself.

"I'd like to tell you that I was good at it. That I trained harder than everyone else, that I passed every test with flying colors. Flying rainbow fish," I paused and allowed myself a brief smile before my face fell again. "But I didn't. I was so angry when I left. Angry at you for making me go, angry at myself for how we left things... It took me weeks before I even tried to participate. I'm pretty sure they considered sending me back to you more than once. Or maybe just murdering me and calling it an accident. Eventually, it was Tatiana who convinced me that I could leave sooner if I just paid attention and learned how to control my powers.

"It was another few weeks, before I was really starting to understand how to restrain my siren's call. How to use it when I wanted to and not use it when I didn't." My voice sounded distant. Far away to my own ears, like murmurs underwater. "We practiced on each other. We weren't supposed to, but Tatiana said she trusted me."

I could see her smiling face before me. The eagerness in her brown eyes as she gripped my hands.

"I don't know why she would trust me; she had only known me a few weeks. I don't know if maybe Marianna had told her something about who I was. How I came to be on land instead of living in the ocean with the rest of them. Maybe she just liked me." I stared at a spot on the floor where the chair leg once had stood. The carpet was an indented circle. I should vacuum that.

"We thought that we were doing a good thing, training together," I said. "Like we'd be done with our time with the others quicker if we practiced outside of the normal training sessions. The sirens from the main pod were mean. Rude to us for being part of Marianna's glamour. Even if we weren't alive during the war, there was still a prejudice, a hatred that Marianna had abandoned them when they'd marched onto land.

"When Tatiana and I worked together, we didn't have to worry about the others. We didn't have to think about them at all. We didn't realize the true reason they didn't want us training with each other." I looked up at the lights above the couch, blinked a few times. "Because the more times you're exposed to a specific siren's call the harder it is to resist them. I didn't feel it. I don't know if it's the strength of my power, or what, but I never felt entirely compelled by Tatiana's song."

Chills raced up my spine of the memory. I stifled a shiver. "Tatiana didn't tell me, but by the time we were done training together she couldn't say no to me."

A sharp hiss, an intake of breath through clenched teeth sounded in front of me. I swallowed hard.

"We had to wait for a final test. It required a sailing vessel, so we had to wait until one was within range of the pod. They sent all six of us out with one instructor to confirm our success. We were supposed to trail the vessel, like the mermaids of old tales luring sailors to their deaths. Our task was to call the sailors one at a time to the edge of the ship and right before they stepped off to push them back —to let them go. No one was supposed to die."

The scent of the ocean hit my senses, salt and brine, as my memories consumed me. I bit the inside of my cheek until it bled. Salt again on my tongue. Just like that day. "I thought I was being clever. I thought I was going to prove that I was better than all of them. I don't know why I did it, some kind of perverse pride taking me over. Some need to prove that those of us from Marianna's glamour were just as melusine as the rest of them. Just as strong." I took a deep breath. "I was so stupid.

"I was the last to try. Only one had failed so far, not even able to get a sailor to come to the railing of the ship in the middle of the night. Tatiana had done beautifully, I guess our hard work had paid off. But I had to do better. It wasn't enough to just succeed, I had to be the best. So instead of raising my voice and singing to a sailor on board, I sang to her.

"I sang to the only friend I had in that entire ocean. I told her to get me a sailor. I think half of me didn't believe that it would work; a small part of me thought that I could just laugh it off as a joke. But when Tatiana began pulling her body up the rope, I knew it was no joke. She hung from the side of the ship her tail transforming into two slender brown legs as she left the water behind. I called her back. I tried; I swear. But I was scared."

I tried to find my father in the room, hoping to make eye contact with his spirit. "That's the first lesson they give us, you have less control over your power when you're scared. Just like you told me about the ghosts. It's funny. The rules are the same. When you're scared you lose control. The rest of us were frozen, as certain as if we had been icebergs floating on the waves. All wide-eyed teenagers as we watched her disappear over the railing.

"Then it was like a spell was broken, I called to her in desperation, begging her to come back. Everyone was yelling, we were going to be seen. So, I turned on them. It was the first time I ever used my power on more than one being at once. I didn't know if I could do it. I took a deep breath, pushed the fear down till I didn't feel it anymore, and I commanded them to stop. Every single melusine in our group fell silent, even the instructor. They stared at me with wide glassy eyes, awaiting my next command. I told them to stay where they were and then I climbed the rope.

"The deck was near empty in the middle of the night, The moon shone down on those wooden planks. That's one image I can't get out of my head," I said, seeing it now. "The way the moon shone on that freshly swabbed deck. There had been one sailor on watch. He stood near the prow of the ship staring out into the water frozen, glassy eyed, like I'd left the melusines in the sea below. I don't know why Tatiana hadn't grabbed him. Maybe she hadn't seen him; maybe she thought I wanted someone else. That had to be it. Certainly it was my taste she was trying to please.

"The rest of the deck was empty, and I knew Tatiana had gone below. It was the most dangerous thing she could have done. If the men saw her, if the sailors tried to catch her, certainly they'd find us all. It would be a bloodbath. I stole down into the hold, blinking as my eyes adjusted to the dark lantern-lit space. My legs tingled, stinging after the recent transformation. It was as if I was stepping on splinters the whole way. I grabbed a blanket off an unoccupied hammock that hung by the stairs and wrapped it around me. The last thing I needed was for the sailors to find a naked woman aboard.

"Tatiana must've been close. I felt sure that if I could find her, I could compel her to stop. At least I hoped so. I hoped that whatever power the siren's call had over her would be reversible. Or at least could be superseded by another order. Most of the men were sleeping, hammocks swinging gently as the sea moved the ship.

"I found her at the end of the first row of men, standing over a hammock where a young man slept. He couldn't have been much older than we were. His hair was blond and stiff with dried salt. She was just staring at him. I didn't know what she was waiting for, but I took my chance. I called her name. I whispered as forcefully as I could, hoping not to wake the men around us. Their snores and foul breath hung in the air pressing on us from all sides. She wouldn't even turn to look at me. I reached forward to grab her hand and she startled. Her movement jostled the hammock before us, and the young man woke up.

"Eyes as blue as any I've ever seen locked on mine. I jumped forward before he had a chance to call out, to wake the others. I clamped a hand over his mouth. He struggled against me and whatever spell I had put on Tatiana snapped as she realized what danger we were in. Together the two of us were able to subdue him and drag him up onto the deck before he had a chance to wake anyone else. When we were top side, I could see in Tatiana's eyes that she wasn't actually free from my orders. She immediately pushed the young man toward me telling me that she got him for me. The look in her eyes was imploring, desperate for my approval.

"I didn't know what to say. We hadn't been taught what to do in a situation like this. I told her that this wasn't what I wanted, and I saw her face shatter. Her eyes filled with tears and before I knew what she was doing she had thrown herself over the edge of the ship into the sea below. That left me standing with the young man, and nothing but a thin blanket between us."

I wished then that Dad was there with me. That I could see him and read his facial expressions. See what he was thinking. The silence, the not knowing, was too hard.

Dad's voice spoke again, from above the coffee table. "Did you kill him?"

I shook my head.

"Did you try?"

"I didn't know what else to do. If he had woken the crew, they would have attacked. We broke all kinds of rules just being on the ship. They would have been justified." I bit my cheek again in hopes pain would force back the lump that rose in my throat, the tears that were stinging my eyes. I hadn't told anyone about this, not even Brigitte. "I attacked before he had a chance to raise his arms. I was going to kill him, a fear I'd never known taking over. My vision went red, I have no idea what I did to him. When I came back to myself, I was beating his head against the foremast. He was covered in blood. I didn't even know if he was breathing when I dove off the side of that ship."

I clasped my hands together in my lap. They were shaking. Blood rushed in my ears, the sound of an ocean wave enveloping me.

"And you think this sailor is Nathaniel?" Dad's voice asked.

"I know it is." I shook myself and took a deep breath. "He practically admitted to me that he was that sailor. He must've never left the ocean, becoming a smuggler himself as he got older. That explains why he was so familiar to me, why I was drawn to him." I dropped my voice low. "Or maybe why he was drawn to me."

"It is possible," Dad's ghost said. "I don't know enough about your siren abilities to know if it would call him to you after all these years, even without him understanding why."

"I understand why he took the amulet. Why he won't trust me to help him. I wouldn't trust me either."

"It certainly makes sense."

I dropped my feet to the floor and crossed my legs before me, reaching out a hand to pat the duffel I had set beside me on the couch. "I don't know what I'm going to do."

"Poincare will understand," Dad said. "He's an asshole, but he's a businessman. He'll let you finish the work you're doing. He just may not pay you as much at the end of it."

"I promised him he'd have his amulet by Monday," I said. "I shouldn't have promised."

A sigh washed over me with a cool touch. "No, you shouldn't have. That was a rookie mistake. You never promise a client anything."

I sat in the silence letting his words settle like a weight on my chest. He was right. That was as close to rule number one as it got in this game. Never make promises.

There was a flutter as a breeze touched the curtains in front of the window to my left. That window was closed. Dad must be pacing over there; his voice came from that direction. "You said amulet?"

"What?"

"When you told Poincare that you would get it to him on Monday, you said amulet?"

I thought back. "Yes, I did."

"Well at least you know you're on the right track," Dad said. "Whatever he lost, it's an amulet."

"That doesn't exactly narrow it down a whole lot," I said.

"Sammy is still out there looking?"

I shrugged. "I don't know. We had a fight."

I heard a smile in Dad's voice when he spoke next. "You're young; you'll fight. But he's a good friend. He's a good man. You'll make up."

Something in my shoulders lifted with relief. I desperately hoped he was right.

I sat for a moment enjoying the silence, the peace of being in the apartment where I grew up. A question burned in my mind though. I knew I had to ask. "Are you upset I took the case? Are you angry that I took Poincare as a client?"

I held my breath. I wanted to reach out with my power to touch his spirit, feel what he was feeling. But I didn't want to invade his privacy, even in death. Finally, he spoke. "I left you in an impossible situation, Meranda. I can't criticize you for the way you picked up the pieces."

I swiped at my cheek. My fingers came away wet. I changed the subject before I would do something really embarrassing like sob. "Sammy's been teaching me to shoot."

"That's good," Dad said. His voice got quiet. "I wish I'd been the one to teach you."

"Did you carry a gun?" I asked.

"I did."

"I don't understand," I said. "You were always so set on preserving life. Even the smallest of lives. How could you carry something that was made to hurt people?"

Dad's voice was soft, thoughtful. "Some people carry a gun, and the world becomes a more dangerous place because of it. Some people carry a gun, and the world becomes safer. I knew what kind of person I was. I would be happy to know that you carried one also. I know what kind of a person you are, Meranda."

"Did you have it?" I asked. "On the night you died? Did you have your gun then?"

Dad's voice sounded farther away although I was sure he was still standing at the same point in the room. I knew the mention of his death would hurt him. I hadn't meant to do that.

"If I had," Dad whispered, "I might still be here."

Chapter Fifteen

Poincare's office looked exactly the same as the last time I was there. But everything was different. The dark leather couches looked black as despair. The low glass table before them threatened to shatter into shards that scraped and scratched. Even the sunlight streaming in the window reflected off the floor with a blinding gleam that attacked any who looked at it.

Or maybe I was being dramatic. Oleksandr rubbing off on me.

I set the duffel bag beside me. It had felt heavy with promise when I'd left this place last, like it held the weight of certain success. Now it was the kind of heavy that could hang around your neck to drown you.

Peggy's nails clacked on the keyboard behind the main desk. She'd asked me to wait, told me that Poincare would call me shortly. The sound of her acrylics beat against my ear drums like a taunting drip of water.

"Miss Haley," the voice came from above me.

I looked up. Poincare stood at the top of the black-railed

staircase. He thought I was bringing his amulet. He was greeting me himself.

I hadn't told Peggy on the phone the real reason I called the meeting. There was no way Poincare could have known that I was here to return the money he had given me.

My brown heels clicked on the glossy stairs as I ascended. They weren't my most expensive pair, they didn't even look the best, but they were comfortable. If I had to eat a large slice of humble pie, I wasn't going to do it in footwear that pinched my toes.

Poincare eyed the duffel. The corners of his mouth turned down ever so slightly. He knew.

"Follow me," he said.

The carpet leading to his office was a dark maroon. Just plush enough to feel expensive. A credenza halfway down the hall made of dark wood stood out from the tan wall. Above it was a painting of an old galleon. Just like the *Sea Wraith* I had seen last week. Funny the things you notice when you're walking to your doom.

Damn, that's Oleksandr again. I have to stop that.

Poincare didn't speak until I had taken a seat on the couch in his office. He closed the door, poured himself a drink, and turned to me.

"What happened?"

"There's no excuse for it," I said. I placed the duffel on the low table before me. "It was my fault. I put faith in bad intel. Your amulet was never there to begin with."

Poincare's breath fogged the inside of the glass tumbler.

"Your money's all here," I said. "I didn't use any of it."

"Do you think that's enough?" Poincare's voice was low. Almost a threat. "Do you think that makes it all okay now?"

"No," I said. I would not be intimidated by him. Even in his office. I had screwed up royally, but I would not be treated like something unworthy of respect. "I understand if you want to fire us. We can hand over any information we found in our investigation. I can give you the names of agencies which may be a better fit."

"This is not about finding a better fit," Poincare hissed. He set the glass down on his desk with a hollow thud and leaned on a fist. The muscles in his forearms rippled as he wrestled with what to say next. "I hired Collier Investigative Agency. I will not break our contract. I did not give you a time limit for your investigation. That was an oversight on my part. As far as we're concerned, you've done nothing to break the agreement we entered into."

"I promised you'd have your amulet by today," I pointed out. A part of me seemed determined to ruin any chance we had of retaining employment.

"That was your mistake," Poincare said. He crossed his arms and leaned a hip against his desk. "But it was not a contract in writing. Perhaps another oversight of mine."

He raised the amber-liquid again to his lips. "I expected more of David Collier's daughter."

I sat in silence and pretended the words didn't sting. He hadn't asked me a question, and I wouldn't try to defend myself. He was right. I should never have made that promise.

"I will give you one more chance," he said finally. "You have one week."

I kept my face neutral. One week to do what we hadn't been able to accomplish in nearly a month. It was almost a guarantee that we would fail. And then, I could expect the reputation of my father's agency to go down with us.

"And this time," Poincare said, pulling out a pen, "I'm getting the agreement in writing."

I signed the document Poincare put in front of me. It

was that or lose all chance of working in the Crescent City. At least now I had a week to figure it all out.

I pulled out my phone as I left Poincare's office.

I had another apology to make.

***

Baxter's bed was again occupied. Seeing the round ball of brown and white fur gave me more relief than I'd like to admit, but I was grasping for good news at this point.

"Where was he last week?" I asked Charlie when the bar's owner came to take my order.

"Sleep study," Charlie said. "I've had customers tell me that he snores. I thought we better check it out."

His tone told me he didn't believe for one second that his perfect angel had a thing wrong with him. The thundering sound from where Baxter slept didn't seem to be enough to change his mind.

I ordered a sparkling water.

Charlie slid a bowl full of pretzels at me 'on the house' and I thanked him.

The bowl was still mostly full when Samuel walked in. He slid onto the barstool beside me and scratched between Baxter's ears.

I had meant to plan a speech. A grand apology that he couldn't refuse, but every time I thought through what I wanted to say, I started making excuses. We sat in silence for a moment. The kind of silence that presses on you. My chest ached with the words I wasn't saying.

"I'm sorry," I said, finally. My voice didn't crack. Victory.

"I shouldn't have left," Samuel said.

I blinked quickly. His words sounded like freedom, but

I wouldn't be caught dead crying in front of him. He'd never let me live it down.

"I should have waited until I heard from you," I said. "I know you hate that I called Oleksandr. I should have talked to you before I brought him in."

Samuel twisted to face me. His brown eyes fixed on mine, drawing me in. "I'm sorry you couldn't get ahold of me. I should have found a way."

His hand touched mine on the bar top. It was a brief contact, a boon that asked for peace between us. I squeezed his fingers, the rough callouses cool and familiar under my touch.

I took my hand back and sipped from my glass.

"You were right," I said. "I shouldn't have trusted Oleksandr's contact without vetting him first."

Samuel's eyes danced in the light of the bare bulbs that hung above the bar. "Say it again," he said. "I don't think I heard you."

I rolled my eyes. "You were right."

"Miracles never cease," Samuel said.

Charlie showed up then with an ale in hand. He placed it in front of Samuel before retreating back down the bar. He'd been listening. Waiting for a break in the conversation to bring the drink. I took up a handful of pretzels.

"What happened?" Samuel asked.

I tried not to grit my teeth. "It was a set up. Nathaniel wanted the amulet for himself. It wasn't even what Poincare had lost. He'd made the whole thing up."

"Damn."

I raised my glass to him. "My sentiments exactly."

"So, you lost the money and the amulet? What did Poincare say?"

"Not the money," I said, frowning. "Nathaniel

somehow talked them out of taking the money. But he got away with the amulet and left us at square one. And I had to give Poincare back his money and tell him what happened."

"That must have stung."

"It was good practice," I said.

"I'm sorry I wasn't there," Samuel said. "I might have stopped it."

I released a long breath. "The more I think about it, the more I realize that Nathaniel didn't want you there. He pissed you off on purpose. If it wasn't his attitude, he would have found another way to get rid of you."

"Yeah," Samuel said. "Still wish I was there."

"Where were you anyway?" I asked.

Samuel took a long sip of his beer before replying. "I called on some of my old contacts," he said. "You know I worked in an anti-smuggling task force with NOPD before—"

I nodded. I knew he wouldn't want to relive what had happened. The mage's fire that destroyed his team. The fact that he'd survived.

"I maintained some contacts after I left," he continued. "They helped with cases I worked with your dad."

"Confidential informants," I said.

"Not exactly," Samuel replied. "They never knew that I was a cop."

"Ah," I said. "Undercover then."

Samuel shrugged.

"No phone when you're undercover."

"Not one that they can trace back to my real life," he said. "I'm sorry, I should have told you. Force of habit to keep it hidden."

"No, I get it."

Samuel sipped his beer. I swirled the pretzel bowl around and watched the last few twists race in a circle. "Next time, maybe, give me the number of your burner phone," I said. "Just in case."

"You got it."

Chapter Sixteen

"Brigitte, I'm coming over," I said.

"Uh," sounded from the other end of the phone.

"Are you not home?" I asked. I blew out a breath and took a left on Paulger. "You're not working today."

"No, I'm home," she said. She trailed off at the end as though she didn't actually want me to come over. Last time she'd sounded like that I had caught her cleaning out her garbage disposal. She was a nervous cleaner. And she hated that I teased her about it.

"Don't bother hiding it," I said. "I know exactly what's going on."

I hung up the phone.

Within seven minutes I was making my way up her front walk.

I pushed open the front door without having to use my key. It was unlocked. We'd have a talk about that later.

"Honey, I'm home," I sang as I walked through the door. It was off key, but it was cheerful. Some might say endearing.

The second I entered her living room, I froze.

"You're not cleaning," I said.

Brigitte sat statue-still her teacup halfway to her mouth.

I looked between her and her guest.

"And you're not alone."

Master Harnock rose, setting a teacup that looked ridiculously small in his large hands down on the coffee table before him. "Meranda," he said.

"Master Harnock," I said. I was sure my face was turning red. Not because of barging in on them, I'd never feel bad about barging into Brigitte's house no matter who was there, but because of how awful my singing was.

Brigitte seemed to recover her composure. "Tea?"

"Sure."

Brigitte poured an extra cup as I took a seat on the couch.

"We may as well continue," Brigitte said. "She knows *exactly what's going on* after all."

I nodded and took the proffered teacup. I had no remote clue why Harnock was here, but if I kept my mouth shut, I could figure it out. I'm a good detective. I run my own agency, dammit.

Harnock cleared his throat. "As I was saying, I don't see any reason why the parents can't speak out at the assembly. The gym has more than enough room and the sound equipment will all be set up."

"Parents are invited to Homecoming," Brigitte pointed out. "It wouldn't be strange to see a few in the audience."

I nodded along and sipped my tea. The protest outside the school gates, a plan to crash homecoming, this integration thing was really getting some momentum behind it.

"How do we keep the Dean from having them pulled

away from the microphone once he realizes what's being said?" Harnock asked.

"Your wrestling team just beat Lafayette High, did it not?" Brigitte asked. "Those boys look up to you. It wouldn't surprise me if some of them had reason to join our side on this even without your say so. You'd have to tell them the truth, though."

The way she said *the truth* made me think there was something I was missing.

"An exercise in playing goalie against a group of school administrators," Harnock said, thoughtfully. "Yes, they might actually enjoy that."

"You do have to consider them just rushing up to the sound booth and cutting off the mics," I said and took a sip of my tea. If I was here, I may as well contribute.

Brigitte tapped a finger on her chin. Her nails were a blue-green and shone like a pearl. They brightened her hazel eyes. I should find her a blouse in that color.

"Jill can take care of that," Harnock said.

Secretary Logan? She normally manned the AV booth. Er, womanned.

"Then it's all settled," Brigitte said. "I'm a part of the Homecoming planning committee anyway. I'll steer them right."

"And I'll talk to the varsity team," Harnock said. "I don't think any of them will be a problem. I think Braden's sister just started manifesting some tendencies toward the magical. He's team captain, the rest will follow him."

"You still need to tell them," Brigitte insisted. A fierceness lit in her eyes. "All in, remember?"

A flush rose on Harnock's cheeks, under the beard. "I will," he said.

I wanted to know what they were talking about so badly I could yell. But I didn't.

When I'd made my way over, I had hoped to find Brigitte alone. I just wanted to complain. Now that Harnock was here, I had different questions.

There was no good segue from the previous conversation. That or whatever Brigitte put in her tea wasn't strong enough to jumpstart my brain into coming up with one. Either way, I had Harnock here anyway, I might as well talk to him.

I set my teacup down and looked up.

"So, Master Harnock, your boy is a dick."

Brigitte's teacup clattered on its saucer. "Meranda," she said. If she wore pearls, she'd be clutching them.

Harnock blinked at me once, unfazed by the accusation. "Artemis is a girl."

"Ha ha," I said. "I'm talking about Nathaniel."

A flash of surprise crossed Harnock's face. I counted it as a victory. I'd never gotten a rise out of him before.

"I know you two are friends," I said. "I saw him when he came to visit you at the Academy."

"Ah," Harnock said. He rubbed a finger along his left eyelid. "He can be a bit abrasive, but I wouldn't call him a dick."

He threw an apologetic look at Brigitte, and she inclined her head.

"Well, he is one," I said. "He almost cost me three hundred thousand dollars."

"I'm sure he had his reasons," Harnock said.

"Had his reasons?" I set my teacup down with a clatter. "How could you assume that? How well do you know him?"

Brigitte cleared her throat, but we both ignored her.

"Well enough," Harnock said. His voice was firm. "I've only ever known him to be a loyal friend. What did *you* do to piss him off?"

I grit my teeth. "It doesn't matter," I said. "He was supposed to be a client. Why do you assume it was my fault?"

"Because I've met you, Meranda."

Brigitte made a sound like she snorted on some tea. I shot her a glare.

"Don't look at me like that," she said. "You barged into my house."

"Do you know him well?" I asked Harnock. "Do you trust him?"

"With my life," Harnock said. "More than once."

"How the hell does a pirate end up befriending a Ranger?"

Harnock hesitated. Turmoil rising behind his eyes. I nearly opened my mouth to compel him to answer me but swallowed instead. I swore I wouldn't use my powers against a friend. Not to be selfish. Not now.

"You don't have to answer," Brigitte whispered. Her slender hand reached over to rest on his knee. It was a comforting touch, familiar.

I blinked.

"I should go," Harnock said.

Brigitte rose with him. "Thank you for coming," she said, following him to the door. She shot me a look when his back was turned.

"Thanks for the tea," Harnock said. He glanced at me. "Meranda."

"See you at training tomorrow," I said sweetly, doing my best to convey that this conversation wasn't over with.

He grunted in acknowledgment and left.

Brigitte closed the door behind him with a soft click and leaned her head against the wood jamb. I could almost hear her silently counting to ten in her head. The urge to call out random numbers to distract her almost overcame me but I pushed it down. I'm a good friend that way.

"What on earth has gotten into you?" Brigitte finally asked, turning to face me.

"I'm an asshole?"

"No—just—gah!"

"You're usually more eloquent than this," I pointed out.

Brigitte took a deep breath. If I wasn't on her last nerve by this time, I was awfully close.

"You were very rude," she said. Her tone was measured, quiet. I almost would have rather she yelled when she was mad, but she hardly ever gave me the satisfaction. It made me feel loud and obnoxious to be near her when she was this way.

"I'm sorry," I said. "I shouldn't have confronted him in your house. I was pissed."

"Obviously," Brigitte said. She walked past me to the coffee table. I helped her clear the dishes and take them to the kitchen. "You owe the swear jar a dollar," she said over her shoulder.

I bit back a grumble. She only enforced the swear jar when she was mad. I dug a crumpled bill out of my pocket and shoved it into the jar that might once have been meant for cookies. It was a gray ceramic, shaped like a cat with painted black whiskers and pointy black ears stuck onto the lid. My dollar landed atop a small mountain of bills, most of which had been placed by me.

A few spare coins clinked against each other on the bottom as I replaced the lid and slid it back on the counter. It joined the small army of ceramic jars that marched across the tile surface, most of them shaped like small household animals. The small brown ferret sitting back on its haunches was the perfect length for spaghetti noodles. A dachshund, whose long body served as both base and lid would open to reveal an unholy number of tea bags. The whole kitchen was whimsical, comforting, from the tea kettle beside the stove whose handle was shaped like butterfly wings, to the dishtowel hung on the oven covered with red and white mushrooms. It was familiar from the time I spent living here when Brigitte and I were in college.

So familiar I didn't feel any hesitancy in opening the cupboard above me and pulling down a glass for water. Often, the glasses in the cupboard were perfectly symmetrical; two sets of four. Something in my brain marked the irregularity of one glass missing. I looked over to where Brigitte was spraying down the teacups. No glass tumbler there. The last time I saw a tumbler out of place was at my dad's laboratory. Where Brigitte had been checking it for the Lycan virus. I hadn't recognized it at the time, but it had been her own glass.

Interesting.

I closed the cupboard. "Hey, do you need to check on your experiment?"

Brigitte made a humming noise. "Day after tomorrow, probably."

"I can be at the Agency to let you in," I said. Sending up a flag of truce. "I think I'll be done at the Academy early that day."

"Sounds like a plan," Brigitte said. "We can walk over together."

She didn't chide me any longer for how I'd treated Harnock. We were back to normal. No tension between us. It was the way we'd learned to survive in this city that hated what we both were, me for my ancestry and she for her magic. We couldn't stay mad at each other for long.

"Do you want to stay for dinner?" Brigitte placed the last cup into the strainer and turned to face me. "It's just leftovers, but there's plenty."

I smiled. "I'd love to."

***

Sammy's call yanked me from my sleep. I was grateful. Even sitting up in bed sweating and shaking while trying to keep my voice steady was better than staring down a nightmare with hands clasped around my throat on the banks of Manchac.

The dream was always the same. It wasn't real. In reality, I had been in the cabin when I had been attacked by Lucy Bettencourt's kidnappers. In the dream, though, I was always on the bank of the swamp. Always almost within arm's reach of the waters that could save me if I could only get to them. Always those waters were too far away.

"Sorry to wake you," Samuel's voice sounded hurried.

"No, it's fine," I said despite my pounding heart. "What's up?"

I pressed a hand to my sternum and squeezed my eyes shut, willing the beating in my chest to slow. Peter Grassi's face floated behind my eyelids, and I snapped my eyes open, tracking my gaze around my empty bedroom. Still empty. He was in prison, not here. He'd never be here.

"I've got something," Samuel said. I could hear the

pounding of a bass line behind him. A girl's voice whooped a little way away from the phone.

"I need a little help getting in," Samuel said. "I'm sure you're teaching tomorrow, but could you—"

"I'll be right there," I said, already half out of the bed. The alarm clock on the bedside table flashed red numbers at me: 02:30. I was going to need a coffee for sure. "Text me the address."

"See you soon,"

I hung up the phone and tossed it onto the tangle of my covers. I tossed clothes around my floor looking for a pair of jeans that wasn't too wrinkled. A black band t-shirt passed the sniff test, and I pulled it over my head. Dark wash jeans followed, and I kicked the pile of clothes aside to find my boots.

If Brigitte saw this place, she'd be aghast. Actually, that might be funny to see. I should invite her over.

A door creaked upstairs, and Marie's chill passed my shoulder in the entryway.

"I'm fine," I said. "Sammy called. It's about the case."

A rush of air moved the curtains in the front room.

"He's not outside," I said. "I'm meeting him somewhere else."

The curtains fell flat. Ever since Samuel had come to rescue me when I was nearly frozen with ghost sickness, Marie had seemed awfully interested anytime he was brought up.

"I hope I'll be back before morning, but I might have to head straight to the Academy," I said.

I don't know why I told her. The house ghost and I typically left each other alone. Since I nearly died in our entryway, I felt a little obligated to reassure her when I left that I was being safe. I'd really done a number on her security, I think. It was like having a sweet, over-protective sister who just happened to be dead. I didn't hate that.

My phone buzzed in my hand, and I looked down to see an address flash onto the screen. That's my cue. I shrugged on the leather jacket that hung on a hook beside the front door.

"Be back soon," I said and pushed out into the cool October night.

The address led me to what was usually a bustling street west of Bourbon. The night life in this part of the city grew more frenzied in the weeks leading up to Halloween. An excitement lit the air along with the smell of stale beer. Fallen leaves mixed with clear plastic cups that once held cocktails, and formed tiny eddies and whirlwinds of discard down the alleyways leading off the street.

At nearly three in the morning, most of the street was deserted. Anyone out this late was either still in a bar partying or hurrying to the safety of home. No one wanted to stay out on the street longer than they had to. Not this close to Halloween. Not during the literal witching hours.

A plastic bottle rattled its way down the sidewalk and knocked against my shin. I picked it up and tossed it into a trashcan.

"Cleaning up the streets?" Samuel's voice asked from an alley to my left.

I suppressed a jump. I had glanced into that alley and hadn't even seen him. "What can I say? It's part of the job description."

His white grin pierced through the darkness. I couldn't help but smile in return.

"Where are we heading?" I asked as he joined me on the main street. His warmth pulsated beside me like a beacon, I wanted to step closer to him. Familiar, like we were in high school again. I held myself back.

Samuel seemed to have no such reservations. The scent of sandalwood graced my nose as he threw one arm around my shoulders. He pulled me against his hard torso, and I let him turn me up the street.

"The club at the end," he said. "They won't let anyone in without a female. Ratios off tonight or something."

I nodded and matched my steps to his. The wool fabric of his black turtleneck was soft under my fingertips as I clasped my hand over the arm that cupped my shoulders. "We aren't exactly dressed for clubbing," I said.

"Easily fixed." Samuel paused and stripped off the sweater. The shirt beneath caught on the hem and I got a good look at chiseled, brown abs before he tugged the white t-shirt down again. Black jeans and a white t-shirt. He could have fit in anywhere. "Men have a far less strict dress code," he said, speaking my assessment aloud.

I glanced at the front of the club. The windows were covered up on the inside with cardboard that had been spray painted black, a white outline of a bat the only marking. The music that poured out to the street consisted of a bass line that sounded as though it would bruise you if you stood too close, accompanied by growling male vocals. This wasn't your typical popular music scene.

A blast of the music barked onto the street as a couple stumbled out of the front door. My brain cataloged them as though I was recalling a witness statement. Male, white, late twenties, around six feet tall, shaved head. A spiderweb tattoo darkened the left side of his neck and led to a dark inked black widow whose legs encircled his skull. He wore a black trench coat that jingled with decorative chains. Matching silver chains hung around the soles of his black platform boots.

The female was shorter, maybe by a half foot. She wore black fishnet stockings and a short leather pleated skirt. Cuts zigzagged across the black checkered t-shirt she wore, showing off pale skin beneath. The man said something to her, and she let out a drunken laugh before pushing her hair back out of her face. Bleached blond hair twisted into locks fell down the left side of her face. The right side of her skull was shaved to the scalp. It too showed off a smaller arachnid counterpart to her partner's. Delightful.

The two of them made their way up the street away from us, boots clomping on the sidewalk in their staggering. I looked down at my black jeans and band tee. Far too boring to fit into the type of club I assumed were behind those doors.

"How good is this lead?"

Samuel's brown eyes were sincere. "Very."

I sighed and pulled the switchblade from the small of my back.

With deft motions I held the fabric of my jeans away from my skin and slashed up and down the thighs. I turned my legs, twisting to look behind me before Samuel took the blade from my hands. I held still as he crouched at the back of my legs and made one long cut behind my right thigh. The cool breeze raised goosebumps on the exposed skin. I was sure the cut reached nearly to my underwear line. I tried to look, and Samuel's hands were warm against my hips as he steadied me. "Almost done," he half-whispered. His voice was husky. My heart beat against my chest.

We'd been this close before. When we'd first met as teenagers, we'd snuck out together a few times before I left for the Gulf and came back a twisted shell of the girl who'd left. Then, I'd pushed him away, too bitter and self-destructive to think about how I might hurt the most gentle guy I'd known. The sound of tearing fabric and I felt the evening breeze against the back of my left calf. I blinked against the memories.

It didn't matter now. It was a waste of time to think about what could have been if I hadn't left him behind to train with the melusines. If I hadn't come back believing I was a murderer. His fingers were light as he placed the closed switchblade in my palm.

"Thank you," I said.

"Anytime." Samuel rubbed a hand on his jeans. I wondered if he was rubbing off the feeling of me. Was he as uncomfortable being close to me as he looked?

"Ready?" he asked.

"One second."

I replaced the switchblade, tucking it low into the waistband of my jeans. The shirt looked too pristine to fit into the kind of club I expected we were walking into, but I wasn't about to cut up the only souvenir I had from the Valkyrie Harts greatest hits tour. I flipped the hem of the shirt up underneath the front and tucked the fabric under my sports bra. Tah-dah. Low-budget crop top.

My torso was corded with muscle from the hours of swimming I had engaged in these last weeks. I touched a hand to my midsection. A small metal bar, pierced through the skin, shone in the streetlights. The ball bearing on the end of it covered where a navel should be. We'd be fine so long as no one looked too closely. The lack of a belly button was hard to explain to the humans. I caught

Samuel staring at me before his eyes found somewhere else to look.

"Shall we?"

Samuel's eyes found mine. "Let's."

The bouncer at the door took one look at the two of us and stepped aside. He didn't ask us any questions, the fact that I was a female enough to get us through.

The music inside was the kind of oppressive that made me want to shove cotton into my ears. Strobe lights flashed around the room, the smell of manufactured smoke from machines near the DJ booth permeated the dancefloor. The lights caught me in the eyes, and I squinted. Had I been out partying all night it would have felt normal. Fresh from bed at nearly three in the morning, it made me want to grind my teeth.

"Who are we looking for?" I asked. I nearly had to yell in Samuel's ear to be heard.

"Bartender," he said. "Black hair, butterfly tattoo. I just needed you to get in, you don't have to work if you don't want to."

"What else am I going to do in here," I yelled over the music. "Sleep?"

Samuel laughed. Damn, I loved the way his eyes crinkled at the corners when he laughed like he meant it.

I held his arm as we crossed the club floor. We dodged gyrating dancers whose chains spun around them like a lethal whirlwind. I stepped too close to one and was rewarded with a stinging slash on my left hip. The place was packed. Halloween exclusive. A pop-up establishment that sprang up for a few weeks and then died out. Its time open was marked with the fierce power of a dying star.

The bar was laid out on the other side of the dance floor, we passed through mostly unscathed. I took a breath of air when we safely landed in front of the raised table laden with plastic cups and cardboard coasters. It was like finally reaching the shore after a harrowing swim in open waters. I eyed a young man with jet black hair who glowered at me from the side of the dance floor. A swim with sharks.

Samuel leaned his elbows on the bar. I turned beside him, facing the rest of the club while he ushered the bartender over.

A raised platform a few feet away from the bar held a dancer contorting her body along with the music. Her slashed black dress barely covered her hips, a view of red panties visible as she lifted her arms above her head. Silver flashed along the sides of her torso, dermal piercings peeking out between the scraps of what was left of her dress. I'd seen this kind of werewolf defense before, but usually it was a part of the garment. Never embedded in a human's skin.

I balled my right hand into a fist as a club patron approached the dancer. A flash of metal and he carried off another scrap of dark fabric. I pictured piranha picking apart their victim. By the end of the night there may not be any part of that dress remaining. I hoped the dancer was being paid well.

Dark eyeshadow hid her eyelids, a swirl of liner leading almost to the corner of her brow. Her eyes closed as she swayed to the music, an almost ethereal quality to her movements. As though she was in a dream. When her eyes opened again, I realized, she was.

A glaze over her eyes turned them a milky gray.

A thrall. Here. This far from the vampire compounds.

I looked around the room. Who ran this place?

"Are you Nell?" Samuel shouted beside me.

I caught a glimpse of the bartender out of the corner of my eye. Straight black hair fell to her waist. Her silver studded belt the only break between her black t-shirt and jeans.

"Who's asking?" She tossed her hair back and I saw the flash of blue inked onto her neck. A monarch butterfly.

Samuel must have seen it too. He flashed a smile that could have disarmed anyone.

"My name's Samuel," he said. "I hear you're the one to talk to if I need something to disappear."

Nell's frown deepened. "I'm not paid to talk. Either order something or step aside."

I guess the disarming smile wasn't working this evening.

"Vodka tonic," Samuel said quickly.

He slid a bill across the counter. I raised an eyebrow. That was certainly more than a vodka tonic normally cost.

Nell tucked the bill into her bra before anyone else at the bar could see it.

"You get one question," she said, setting a blue cup on the counter and pulling out bottles.

Be smart, Sammy. Unless you have a wad of fifties in your pocket, you have one shot at this.

"Did you organize the crew that knocked off Janus Poincare's ship three weeks ago?"

Damn, Sammy. Subtlety not your strong suit, huh?

A smirk contorted the side of Nell's face. "Nope, here's your drink."

From the smell of it, that glass was mostly tonic.

Samuel took a sip from the cup and made a face. "One more question."

"I have other customers to serve," Nell said, turning away.

"Wait," Samuel said. He snaked out a hand and caught the bartender's shoulder.

"I said, I have other customers to serve," Nell warned, her voice raising. Even with my back turned I could hear the threat.

To my right, the thrall stopped dancing. Milky white eyes focused on my partner.

Shit.

It was Nell's.

I sent a quick glance around the club. I didn't know if Nell was the only vampire here. Surely, this was her only thrall, but who knows how many others were in the club. If Sammy kept this up, he'd get us both killed.

I spun around and elbowed him in the side. "You heard her," I said, putting a drunken slur in my voice. "Take a hint, buddy."

Samuel turned to face me. Two seconds was all it took for him to catch on to what I was doing. A slow uptake, if you ask me, but he made up for it with enthusiastic participation. Ice cold vodka tonic splashed over my shirt. The plastic cup landed at my feet with a hollow clatter.

"Whatever," Samuel said, hunching his shoulders and turning away. "You're all assholes."

I peeled the shirt off my chest with my thumb and forefinger. It adhered back to my skin as soon as I let go.

"Here." Nell thrust a handful of napkins at me.

"Thanks," I said. I dabbed at my shirt, but the fabric was soaked. Poor Valkyrie Harts.

"Can I get you anything?" Nell asked. "On the house."

"Oh uhm—" I looked at the folding table filled with half empty liquor bottles. "What's your specialty?"

Nell laughed. It was a more gentle sound than I expected. I caught a glimpse of small, pointed fangs. "I'm a bartender-for-hire," she said. "My specialty is flirting for tips."

I smiled along with her. "Honestly, the soaked shirt is pretty sobering. How about a pick me up."

"You got it." Nell threw me a wink.

I picked the plastic cup of the floor and tossed it into the barrel trashcan beside the bar.

No other patrons flocked to the bar. I found a stool near the end of the long bar top and sat down.

Nell placed a cup in front of me. "Try that."

I took a sip. "Cranberry soda?"

"With orange," Nell said.

"Thanks," I said. I pulled a crumpled bill from my pocket, but she waved me off.

She pulled a stool up on the other side of the bar. "Sorry about your shirt."

I sipped my drink. "It'll dry."

"Why'd you step in back there?"

I shrugged. "I don't like it when assholes won't take no for an answer."

Nell lifted a glass to her lips. "Same," she said. Her eyes lit with a dark fire.

A strangely fierce sentiment from someone who controlled a human against her will. I glanced at the thrall dancing again on its platform.

Her guard was down. I had to press now before more thirsty customers came over.

"He acted like he knew you," I said. "Has he bothered you before?"

"Never seen him a day in my life," Nell said. "I get that a lot."

I sipped my drink, silently urging her to continue.

"It's the tattoo," she said, finally. "Property of Clan Montrose."

"Property," I repeated back to her.

Nell narrowed her gaze. "Once," she said. "No more."

It wasn't uncommon for vampires to leave their clan. Very few of the clans stayed together these days, most of them disbanding in order to fit into Crescent City society. Clan Keiran alone maintained its hold on the strict traditions of their past. As far as I knew, only Oleksandr had escaped them.

I wasn't familiar with Clan Montrose. They can't have been too influential in the city. That or they were very, very careful.

"He was probably looking for my sister," Nell said. "She's the one out there causing trouble."

"A case of mistaken identity," I murmured. "She looks like you, then."

Nell laughed again. "Oh, she's much prettier than me. She's a pureblood."

My heart turned to ice. Why couldn't we be looking for the nice, gentle, half vampire before me?

A man sporting a black mohawk and enough metal studding from his face to be confused with a bristle brush walked up to the bar.

Nell rose. "Besides, Hesta wouldn't be caught dead in a club like this," she said. "Ever since she found a Firestone she's been far too important to tend bar with me. Asshole should have tried *The Thorn.*"

"Sorry," I said. My heart pounded. Now we had a name, a clan, and a location. I would trade a dry shirt any day for intel like that.

Nell shrugged. "C'est la vie."

I downed the last of the drink, savoring the tang of the orange and dropped the cup in the trash.

I found Samuel outside the bar. He was in the black turtleneck again, nearly blending into the shadows outside of the building.

"What did you get?"

I zipped up my leather jacket, covering the soaked shirt against the chill. "Plenty," I said. "But you're not going to like it."

"Oh yeah?"

"Vampires."

"Shit."

I told him what Nell had revealed.

"Have you heard of *The Thorn* before?"

"Nope," Samuel said. "But I can poke around, see what comes up."

I crossed my arms over my chest. Three AM wind sucked.

"What's a Firestone?" I asked.

"No idea, too bad we lost our magical artifacts expert."

I gritted my chattering teeth, but Samuel's eyes danced with humor.

"Maybe Oleksandr will know," I said. The humor left Samuel's eyes and I grinned at him.

"Thanks for playing along back there," I said.

"Not gonna lie, I was still kind of pissed at you," he said. He eyed my next shiver. "I feel much better now."

I barked out a laugh and shivered again.

"Come here," Samuel said. "Let's head back to the Agency."

I tucked myself under his arm and we fell into step. I was grateful that he kept me warm despite the newly acquired holes in my clothes. Despite the soaked shirt I had totally deserved.

I could get used to having him around.

"Let's not fight again," I said. The words fell out of my mouth before I could stop them.

"Deal."

Chapter Seventeen

I ducked under Harnock's fist and dropped hard onto the gymnasium floor. Dammit. My knee throbbed at me as I pushed off. The master-at-arms wasn't the type to let an advantage slide. He turned and tackled me from my half-crouched position. Together we sailed over the basketball court for a half a moment before crashing into the floor again.

I twisted as soon as we landed, wrapping my legs around his torso just as he had taught me, controlling his distance from my face. A flurry of fists came down toward me. I put my arms up, guarding my head. I was sure bruises peppered my forearms already. We couldn't stay this way much longer. I had to do something.

My head dodged the punches, my abs screaming at me with the abuse they were taking. Swimming in a bayou can't quite compare to the demands of lifting your upper body from the ground and twisting from side to side. Finally, I caught his rhythm, dodged his next punch, and bolted upward, wrapping my arms around his head and shoulders.

Before he could throw me off, I slithered behind him,

quick as an eel and had him in a headlock. Ha! I'd never done that before. The victory was short-lived as a massive hand wrapped around my face and pulled me off him as easily as though I was a rag doll. Again, I was flying through the air, the wind cooling the sweat of my brow before skidding along the gym floor. My elbow stung where I was sure a road rash was forming, but I ignored it and staggered to my feet.

Harnock rose from where he knelt and clapped twice. "Much better," he called out. "But not good enough."

Shit.

In a flash he was before me. I raised my hands, warding off his first few punches before responding with a jab and follow up of my own. Sweat dripped down, setting my eyes stinging. My breath came ragged, my lungs burning at the effort to keep my muscles moving. His blows were pushing me back across the floor. A few more moments and I'd be against the bleachers, tripping over them, falling. I couldn't let that happen. With a cry that tore from somewhere deep in my chest I lunged at him, pushing both of my bruised forearms into his torso. Pushing him back just far enough that I could raise a foot. I planted the boot into the center of his chest and bounced off.

Dammit. It was as bad as hitting the barred door in the underground market. I tucked my chin before I landed on the ground again, but the impact still took my breath away. I lay for a moment, two, gaping up into the harsh artificial lights. The patches of sky visible through the windows in the ceiling criss-crossed with fluffy white clouds. I took a deep breath as my lungs expanded again and coughed twice.

"That was good thinking," Harnock said. He stood above me, extending a hand down to help me up. "Next time, plant your foot stronger. You have to have a solid base for a kick like that."

I let out an unladylike grunt as he hauled me to my feet. My whole body was sore. I couldn't tell what was worse, the bruises on my forearms, the scrape on my elbow, or the wounded pride of knowing that I'd almost stood a chance this time and had still failed.

I collapsed onto a bleacher and took two gulps of water.

"Hey," Harnock said. "You're getting better. When we first started training together you couldn't last half that amount of time. Your stamina is improving."

"Thanks," I said. "I've been working on my cardio."

Harnock turned away with a snort and started packing up his sparring gear. I tore the Velcro on my gloves and stripped them off as well. Despite the gloves, my knuckles were split and bleeding. I bent my elbows to admire the smattering of bruises on my forearms, already turning from red to purple.

"You should have Brigitte take a look at those," Harnock said. "No reason you need to walk around looking like an overripe banana."

That was a lovely image. "Thanks," I said.

Brigitte had told him her secrets, her powers. A protective instinct in me reared up, but I pushed it back. She was a big girl. She could tell whomever she wanted.

"Why are you so focused on helping her?" I shoved my gloves into my gym bag. "Her dream of a united school, magical and nonmagical beings attending classes together. The Dean will never stand for it. Why encourage her?"

"Some dreams are worth fighting for," Harnock said. "No matter how much of a long shot they seem to be."

A fortune cookie answer. How very guru of him.

"She's your best friend," he said. "Why aren't you helping?"

The words stuck like tiny barbs in my heart. Like an accusation that I had already told myself not to listen to.

"It's not that simple," I whispered.

"For me, it is." Harnock said. He lifted his gym bag.

"What's your secret?" I asked quickly, before he had a chance to leave. "Why are you so invested in this?"

Harnock rubbed a knuckle into one eyelid. "Frankly, Meranda, if you're not involved. It's none of your business."

I bit back a retort as my phone rang.

"Meranda Haley," I said into the receiver.

"Meranda," Nathaniel's voice. Drawn, desperate. "You have to help me."

"I most certainly do not," I snapped and hung up the phone.

"Who was that?"

"It's Nathaniel," I said. "He's been calling almost nonstop all morning."

The phone rang again. I checked the caller ID and slid it into my bag. Not Sammy with a lead, I don't need to answer, I told myself.

"You're not going to pick up?"

"If he needed my help, he shouldn't have screwed over my case. Poor foresight on his part. Besides, he has the answer to all his problems without me. He made that perfectly clear."

I ignored the pull in my chest. Could I really just treat him that way when he had once been a client? An asset? When I had hurt him so badly already?

My phone buzzed twice, and a text came through. *Amulet not working. Plz help.*

He couldn't even take the time to spell out the word

'please'? I looked up into Harnock's hard eyes and gave him my best unbothered smile.

I finished packing my gym gear and zipped the bag closed.

The phone rang again. I envisioned chucking it across the gym floor.

Harnock's voice rumbled. "I really think you should pick that up."

"Frankly, Geoff," I spit his words back at him, "it's none of your business."

"He's a friend," Harnock ground out.

I held the ringing phone up on the palm of my hand. "Remind me, how is it that a Ranger and a pirate end up friends?"

I could feel that I was close to his secret. If I pressed a little farther, maybe I'd get something out of him. I leaned forward as Harnock opened his mouth. Closed it again.

Dammit, I was so close.

Harnock turned on his heel and stalked across the gym floor, his boots a muffled thud. Just before he disappeared out the double doors, I saw him put his own phone to his ear.

I was just standing, placing my bag on my shoulder, when those double door slammed open again. "Meranda, you have to help," Harnock's voice boomed.

My heart jumped. It couldn't be that serious, I told myself. He had a protection amulet, after all.

"Meranda, let's go!"

I walked across the gym toward him. A deafening silence descending on my ears. "Combat training's over," I said, sweetly. "You don't get to give me orders anymore."

"Please," Harnock said. I'd never before seen the wild look that entered his eyes.

I crossed my arms.

"I'll tell you whatever you want to know," he said. "Just please help him. He'll die."

A chill crawled down my spine. "Fine," I said. "Where is he?"

"We'll take my truck," Harnock said.

"Then you talk on the way."

"I was working a case with the Rangers," Harnock said, "somewhere north of the Louisiana border. It was a wasteland out there. Only a few farmers and loners who had formed into small towns to watch out for each other. The Wilds are dangerous, most humans have to flock together to survive. People had started disappearing a few weeks before we were called in. Livestock turning up butchered, shit like that."

Harnock took a hard right as we left the neighborhoods surrounding the Academy and headed west. I grabbed the handle above the door and held on. Our gym bags thumped together as they slid across the back bench seat.

"Normally, the Rangers wouldn't take a case like that. The pay's no good. But the de facto leader of the settlement had some family tie to our captain. That guaranteed our involvement."

Another sharp turn and I braced my feet against the floorboards. I wasn't one to get seasick, but the thought definitely flashed through my mind. When it isn't a life-or-death situation, I made a mental note to never drive with Harnock again.

"Nathaniel was there, among the settlers. He'd only arrived a few months prior. Kept to himself. Honestly, half the settlement thought he was the cause of what was going on. We'd only been there a few days before the truth came out."

Harnock glanced down at his phone, tapped the screen once to redisplay the text message that directed us. I squeezed my eyes shut. That would keep us from hitting something, right?

I unclenched my fists as Harnock returned his eyes to the road.

"What was it?"

Harnock clenched his jaw, a white scar stood out under his short brown beard. "Werewolves.

"We only figured it out when the people who had gone missing came back. They tried to convince us that they had their shift under control. That they weren't a danger to the town." Harnock rubbed at his left eye, the white of it reddened with irritation. "That only lasted about two days. We ran them out of town. Hoped that they would find somewhere else to haunt, but new wolves are unpredictable. Unmanageable. It didn't take long before we had no choice but to fight them off."

"They had formed a pack?"

"There was an alpha already," Harnock said. The truck bounced over a pothole, and he made a hissing noise through his teeth. "Maybe two original pack members. He turned the settlers to expand his control over the region. Extend his territory farther."

"Nathaniel helped you?" I asked. "That's why you trust him so much?"

"Nathaniel's the one who figured out what was going on in the first place," Harnock said. "If it weren't for him warning everyone, we would have lost far more settlers to the wolves than we did. As it was, the Rangers came through mostly unscathed."

"He saved your life," I said. The picture starting to come together in my mind.

"More than once," Harnock said. "During the defense of the town, I was bitten. There was no knowing if I would turn or not. It was protocol to wait it out, to see if I would remain human. But I knew they were debating whether to be preemptive in their strike. No one wanted to wait until the next full moon to find out what would happen.

"In the end, Nathaniel stayed with me even after the settlement turned against me... Even after the rest of the company left."

I eyed the scar on the side of his face. It descended below his jaw line, along his neck. If I wasn't this close to him, I wouldn't even have noticed it beneath his beard.

"What happened?" The question came out nearly a whisper.

"They ran us out of town," Harnock barked a laugh. "No one wanted to deal with the ticking time bomb living among them, and Nathaniel wouldn't let me go alone. They left him with a pistol with a single silver bullet."

Harnock's throat bobbed as he swallowed hard.

"You're still here," I said.

Harnock nodded. "I'm still here. But I might not have been. Had they given me that pistol, run me out of town alone... I may not have taken the chance."

A lump hitched in my throat. Nathaniel didn't have to stand by him. Didn't have to go with him. Whatever drove him out of the ocean and sent him into the wilderness hadn't hardened him so much that he wasn't still willing to help a stranger. I tried to square the story with the version of Nathaniel I'd seen.

I couldn't.

But that was my fault.

"We're here," Harnock said. He slammed on the brakes. I braced my forearms on the dash and prayed the airbags wouldn't go off.

The truck stopped near the end of a dead-end road. We were outside the city, where asphalt turned to dirt. Just before the car was a metal structure blocking off the rest of the road. Cyprus trees rose on either side, casting shade over the dirt and allowing only mottled sun beams to come through the canopy.

"Where's here?"

"This is the location he gave," Harnock said, shoving his door open. "Do you see him?"

I hopped down from the cab and scanned the trees. "I don't see anything."

"Nate!" Harnock yelled. He cupped his hands around his mouth, amplifying his voice. "Nate, where are you?"

The hairs on my arms prickled upright. There were always spirits lingering in the swampland outside the city. Victims of the swamp itself or other humans or what had crawled out of the portals to wreak havoc on this world. I closed my eyes and reached for them.

I could feel something. A mass of something to our right, or maybe ahead, two o' clock maybe. Just as when working with Marie, it was like trying to discern an unfamiliar shape through a thick glove. I had gotten into the habit of keeping my shields up as a default. If I wanted to know where Nathaniel was, I had to lower them.

I dropped my shields.

Claws flashed through my mind.

Shit.

I slammed the shields back into place and gripped the

sides of my head. A pounding took up residence in my skull. Like the worst hangover I'd ever had. I could barely open my eyes, the light throbbed.

"Go right," I gasped. I raised a hand and pointed. "That way, he's close."

I had to assume the spirits were with him. He was what they wanted.

One hand over my brow to shield my eyes from the light, I yanked open the truck door and reached into my gym bag. Iron knuckles brushed my fingertips as I found the correct pocket. I pulled them onto my hands and turned to go. But the light glinted off something on the floorboards.

Oh yeah, that was even better.

I followed the sound of Harnock calling Nathaniel's name. The throbbing in my skull eased. At least it was temporary. I was never lowering my shields again. I watched the dirt in front of me. There was no way I'd let Harnock find me stuck in the bayou mud trying to catch up.

"Nathaniel!" Harnock's tone changed. He'd found him.

I ran.

I shoved long grasses and tree branches out of my way. A sharp branch whipped my face. I pushed it aside and found them.

Harnock stood before Nathaniel's crumpled form. The pirate was covered in blood, his clothes torn, and one arm bent wrong at the elbow. My eyes swept past quickly, but I could tell he was barely breathing.

My heart clenched.

I'd left him looking like that before.

Beyond Harnock, standing before him like a menacing army, were six spirits.

"You can see them?" I shouted.

Harnock didn't turn toward me, keeping his eyes on the threat. "Yes, I can see them. What the hell are they?"

I looked them over as I crossed the clearing. They seemed surprised that they were visible. Surprised that they had resistance. They stood frozen, eying us both, seeming unsure what to do.

Most of them wore torn and ragged cotton slacks and loose shirts. Two were naked from the waist up, even in their ghostly state I could still make out the sun-tanned sheen of their skin.

The foremost spirit, the one closest to Harnock, sported a wide-brimmed hat with an elaborate feather sticking out of the top. With the straggled mass of hair coming from his chin and the murderous glint in his eyes, he looked like nothing so much as an old illustration of Blackbeard the Pirate.

Six spirits. I couldn't take on six at once. Not when they were this angry.

"Ghosts," I whispered as I stepped up beside Harnock. "Nathaniel's being haunted."

Harnock made a humming noise beside me. That was the only inclination that he had to wrestle with the information he'd been given. I passed him the metal bar I'd grabbed from his truck's floorboards.

"Iron," Harnock said, thoughtfully. "Very good."

"As soon as you get a chance," I said, softly, "you swipe through as many of them as you can, grab Nathaniel and run. I'll catch up."

I'd expected some level of protest. Some kind of 'what about you?' or 'I'm not leaving you behind', but Harnock simply nodded.

The foremost ghost spoke. "You are interfering in our

business." His voice was as ragged as his beard. Choppy, like he spoke through a torn throat. "Leave now."

"Can't do that," I called out. "You attacked a friend. He is under my protection."

I raised my voice. Command lacing my tone. "Begone."

The sailors behind the captain flickered once, but whatever power held them to this plane, I couldn't touch. What the hell? This was my literal job.

The pirate laughed. Like a cheap movie villain. Are you kidding me?

"You can't touch us, *Potesta*." He spat out my title as though it left a bitter taste in his mouth. He spoke to the sailors that flanked him. "Get Nathaniel and get back to the wraith. Kill them both if they try to stop you."

A chill rippled through my gut at his words.

I reached out with my powers. Straining to feel them with my shields locked in place. I grabbed at the sailors behind him, but they slipped through my grasp as easily as if they'd been slicked with grease. Again, what the hell?

My mind screamed at me, and I struggled to keep my face neutral. I couldn't touch them. If I couldn't command them, I couldn't control them. The iron crowbar beside me twitched as Harnock tightened his grip on it. We were going to have to fight them.

"I give you one last chance," I said. "Go before you don't have a choice anymore."

One sailor with torn black pants and a scar that cut across his chest spoke up. "Not without our captain."

Fine. My heart beating in my ears, drowned out all other sound. They wouldn't leave without their captain. I'd take him out first.

I was about to step forward, to start the fight when a soft

touch on my ankle stopped me. I looked down to see Nathaniel's hand weakly grasping at my leg.

"Please," he whispered. Blood bubbled from between his lips.

"I'm getting you out of here," I told him. "Just hold on."

His fingers fell away from me. Exhausted. We didn't have long.

The captain took advantage of my distraction and lunged for me. I ducked under his arms and tackled him around the middle. We crashed into the soft ground and rolled. He maintained his corporeal form long enough to punch at my face. I dodged to the side, but a good swipe still landed on my cheek. It was like a hammer blow. I let out a growl and drove both fists coated in iron into his gut. He let out a whoosh of unholy air and I landed two blows on his face before he disappeared.

I staggered to my feet to see the hulking form of Harnock holding off the other spirits. The old Ranger seemed bigger than normal as he swung the crowbar like a baseball bat, cutting through any sailor who got too close. As the bar passed through them, the ghosts disappeared, banished from our plane to regroup somewhere else. They weren't really gone, I knew. Whatever damage the iron did, it couldn't get rid of them permanently.

Only my powers could do that. Or, at least, my powers were supposed to.

Two sailors broke off from the group as they saw me on my feet. I raised my fists. Come on, assholes. Let's do this.

Still out of reach, they turned. They moved toward the crumpled form on the ground.

No, no, no. Shit, no.

I ran for them, throwing myself before them and back-handing the left one across the face. He staggered back a few paces and the other sailor grabbed at my arms. I snarled as his chilled grip encircled my wrist.

The iron froze on my knuckles, burning my skin. I raised my other fist and jammed it into his face. Again, and again, and again. Until he let go with a howl and disappeared.

Harnock was at my side. His breath coming like a jagged growl.

Two sailors remained. They regrouped across the clearing, looking at each other with wide eyes, trying to gauge when to attack next.

"Give me the crowbar," I said. "Get Nathaniel to the truck."

Harnock made a frustrated noise beside me.

"Now," I said. "I've got this!"

I kept my eyes on the two threats and pushed him back. His arm was warm and hard under my touch. And—furred?

A chill touched my chest. I looked at him.

Yellow eyes met mine, glinting in the light that drifted through the trees. His face had elongated, a snout pressing out where his nose and mouth had been. Gray fur covered his face and arms. At the end of his hands, claws closed around the crowbar.

Werewolf.

I quelled the panic that rose in my throat. He'd fought alongside me. This was Harnock, I told myself. Friend.

"Take him," I whispered, my voice close to shaking. "Keep him safe."

I took the iron bar from his grasp, suppressing a shudder as my hands brushed against claws that were the length of my index finger.

The hybrid blinked once and turned. I stepped before him and fixed my eyes on the two sailors across the clearing.

They tracked Harnock's movements behind me. I heard a moan as he lifted Nathaniel, heavy footfalls as Harnock moved away.

The sailors must have decided I was easy prey without the werewolf at my side. Big mistake.

They ran together, but the one on the left reached me first. Sunlight glinted off the gold rings in his ears.

I swung the iron in a wide arc, and he leapt back.

His friend reached me a second later. I twisted away from his grasp and punched out with my iron knuckles.

The attack paused as the two spirits stood side by side, regarding me silently. I couldn't let them think this through too carefully. Force of habit made me reach toward them with my powers again, feeling them out. This time, for some reason I could touch them. I could feel them.

I wasn't about to question a gift. I dipped deep into my well of power.

"You don't have to do this," I said. Distracting them while I worked.

I drew my powers around them like a net, not quite forcing my will on them yet, but fencing them in.

"You can go to your friends of your own accord. I don't have to be the one to send you there."

Another glance passed between them. I wove my powers together behind them, like a drawstring threading through the net I'd made.

I could see the moment they'd decided. The moment they thought to themselves that I was only one small human, and they could take me.

They took one step forward.

I drew the net closed with a snap and they disappeared.

Pain exploded behind my eyes, and I hit the ground. I

cradled my head in my hands. What was happening? Why were my powers reacting this way?

A moan escaped my lips.

Why wouldn't it stop?

I whimpered as I felt strong arms beneath me. Gray fur pressed against my cheek. My head throbbed with each step we took out of the bayou. The worst stab of pain came when I sneezed.

Harnock placed me in the front seat of the truck, and I pressed my head between my knees, willing the pain to stop. He started the engine with a rumble, and I heard a groan from the backseat.

Nathaniel.

I snapped my head up, pain forgotten, and twisted to see him.

He held his broken left arm tightly across his chest. His face was a beaten mess of blood and torn skin. His lower lip was nearly ripped clean off, white teeth stained with red beneath. Both eyes had swollen shut and his blond hair plastered to his forehead with dirt and blood.

The ghosts had beaten him near to death.

"Brigitte's," I said. "We have to get him to Brigitte."

"Way ahead of you," Harnock said.

I turned to see him human again. His perfectly normal hands gripped the wheel. No trace of claws left.

He gunned the gas, and we lurched forward. I rolled over the bench seat and landed on the floor beside Nathaniel's seat, bracing his body with my own. I pulled the seatbelt over us both.

This was going to be a bumpy ride.

Chapter Eighteen

We left Harnock's truck in the street parking in front of Brigitte's house. Brigitte met us at the door, Harnock carrying the mangled body up her front walk. I trailed behind, scanning my eyes up and down the street. We hadn't seen a trace of the ghostly sailors who had attacked Nathaniel since we left the clearing, but if they were drawn to him, Brigitte's house wasn't protected. We'd need to move him quickly.

Up until finding Nathaniel, I had felt righteous indignation. I had felt completely justified ignoring his calls. He'd fired me from his case, he'd betrayed my trust and wasted my time. But now, watching Harnock set Nathaniel's barely recognizable body down on the surface of Brigitte's surgical table, a fluttering took up residence in my gut. It felt cold and hollow, the sinking sensation of guilt.

Brigitte stepped up to the table, her hands already taking on a warm golden glow. "What are we dealing with?"

"I-I didn't do a full catalog of injuries," I stammered. My brain filled with fuzz. I couldn't think straight. I should have checked him over. I should have more to give. "He's human, I think. Fully human." I paused.

"What did this?" Brigitte asked. Her words clipped, all business.

"Spirits," I said. I couldn't keep the uncertainty out of my voice. "Spirits from the sea."

"On land?" Brigitte asked, but she didn't pause her work. It was a question that pulled me up short, too. How did spirits from the sea end up this far inland? Why were they tied to Nathaniel?

Brigitte's patient moaned on her table, and I rushed forward. He raised his hands as he came to, as though to fight off an incoming attack.

"You're safe," I said quickly, taking his hands in my own. "You're safe now. We've got you."

Nathaniel's body bucked on the table. He tore his hands from my grip with a cry. "No," he yelled and over again. "No! No!"

Harnock pushed me aside and grabbed the hands that now swung toward Brigitte.

"It's me," he said, his deep voice a low vibration through the room. "It's me, Nathaniel. Hold still. We're fixing you up."

Nathaniel relaxed at the sound of his friend's voice. Even with his eyes swollen shut, he still knew to feel safe when that voice was near. Not like mine.

I drifted back away from the table. Unmoored and unneeded. My hands tingled and I rubbed them on my thighs. When I looked down, my hands were stained red, and my pants darkened with blood.

Brigitte's voice was soft as she addressed Harnock. "I need you to hold him as still as you can. I don't have the power reserves to keep him unconscious and heal his injuries, it will take too much."

I stayed long enough to see Harnock's nod of understanding before I left the room. My stomach roiled in my gut.

My fault, I thought. It was my fault.

The first screams reached my ears as I hit the hallway.

I did that. *Myfaultmyfaultmyfault.*

I wanted to throw my hands over my ears, plug them with wax like this was a Grecian legend. But I didn't. I deserved every ounce of the agony that drove into my heart with each scream. I sank down the wall until I hit the floor, my legs pulled up to my chest. I leaned my head back and closed my eyes. Wincing with each cry, but not moving.

I wouldn't leave him.

Not in his agony.

Not again.

The hall where I sat was as near to the center of the house as I could get. I extended my shields, pushing them like a balloon inflating around me. I stretched them to the edges of the house. If the ghosts were coming, I would know about it. I couldn't heal him like Brigitte could. I couldn't comfort him like Harnock. But this I could do. An ache bloomed behind my eyes, and I gritted my teeth against it.

Brigitte emerged from the room less than a half hour later. My legs had fallen asleep, needles of pain stabbing into me as I extended them. I drew the shield back to myself. If the ghosts hadn't shown themselves by now, I hoped they were having trouble finding us. I couldn't maintain the shields on the house. I had to call Florentina.

"He'll be fine," Brigitte whispered. She dropped a hand to my cheek, and I leaned into it.

"Your turn."

"It was my fault," I said. I choked on the last word and squeezed my eyes against their stinging.

Brigitte cupped my chin and lifted my face to hers. "Then make it right."

She didn't offer me pat answers. She didn't try to assure me that I'd done nothing wrong. She wouldn't insult me that way. Just, make it right.

I nodded. She helped me to my feet and supported me to the living room couch. I hadn't realized until then just how exhausted I was. How badly my legs ached. Brigitte let out a sigh as we both sank onto the couch, facing each other.

"You must be tired," I said, pushing her hands away. "Go rest."

Brigitte pressed her face close to mine. The front of her hair had come undone, dark coils springing around her face. Dark shadows deepened under her hazel eyes. A tense pull lengthened the corners of her mouth, but she quirked it up into a smile. "Let me take care of you."

I would have protested again, but I was too drained. I nodded and closed my eyes. The light of her hands cast an orange glow behind my eyelids as she began to work. My face tingled as she repaired the bruises, her tender touch running over my cheekbones. Her hands ran along my shoulders and down both arms, raising my hands out in front of me as she healed the bruises on my forearms, the scrape on my elbow. Pressing against my temples, she eased the ache in my head, leaving behind only the feeling of exhaustion. Finally, she stopped with a sigh.

I opened my eyes to see the shallow grooves on her face deepening. The hair at her temples fading to a dull gray.

"You've done too much," I said. "You need sleep."

Brigitte nodded, her mouth widening into a yawn.

"Thank you," I said. Pulling her up and walking her toward her bedroom. "Now go to bed."

Brigitte walked to her room as though she was leaden down with a ton of bricks. Her feet nearly shuffled on the floor before she collapsed on the bed. I crossed the room and rolled her under the covers. She gave me one last sleepy smile before she turned away and slept.

I tiptoed out of the room and up the hall, pausing before her small clinic room. My feet felt glued to the floor as I struggled with the question of whether to go in and check on Nathaniel or not. I jumped as the door opened, startling me out of my thoughts.

Harnock peeked a head out. "I have to call Artemis, tell her I'll be late," he said. "Can you watch him a moment?"

I nodded and swallowed against a dry throat. He held the door open for me and I stepped in, trying not to show him my hesitation.

Nathaniel lay on the examination table, his left arm across his chest, whole and healed. His eyes were closed, no longer swollen shut, but resting. His chest rose in even breaths. The bruises were gone, but the blood remained, staining all that I could see.

Brigitte had cut his shirt away. Harsh slashes across his ribs and shoulders were now sealed, but the seam rose red against his tanned skin. I fought back the lump in my throat.

Make it right.

I warmed water in the sink and filled a basin. Brigitte kept towels and wash cloths in the cabinet above the sink, and I dropped a small white cloth into the water. I pulled a tray table to Nathaniel's side and placed the basin atop it.

His hair was crusted with blood, blond color almost inscrutable beneath the red. I placed a towel on the examination table, curving it around his head to catch any drips and began to clean his skin.

It was slow going. I had to refill the basin more than once before his face was clean. I moved to his hands next, some part of me wishing he was awake and could squeeze my fingers back as I worked on him. The skin of his palms was rough beneath my touch, calloused. I patted him dry with the towel, careful not to rub against the fresh scars. I remembered how sensitive that new skin was.

Without thinking, my hand drifted to my chest. The new skin that Brigitte had crafted to cover the burns there. Nathaniel had touched it when he met me at Baxter's. Just reached out and placed a finger on my chest as though it was the most natural thing in the world. If my siren-song still carried him to me after all these years, maybe it was.

I poured the reddened water down the sink and rinsed out the basin, wishing I could as easily rinse the foul taste out of my mouth. My song had nearly killed him. It was a curse that brought him back to me.

Harnock returned, a cup of coffee in his hand. "There's a fresh pot," he said.

I nodded and draped a clean white sheet over Nathaniel's torso. He deserved the dignity of full covering.

I could use a cup of coffee.

Harnock joined me in the living room a few moments later. He refilled his coffee cup from the pot in the kitchen and sank into an armchair beside the couch. I sipped my coffee, grateful for the warmth that spread through my chest as I swallowed.

"Should someone—"

"He's a big boy," Harnock said. "He doesn't need us to hold his hand while he sleeps."

I tried not to stare at his fingers that wrapped around the small mug. Less than an hour before, those had been claws.

"He stayed with you?" I asked. "Through your first change, I mean."

Harnock nodded. "I don't think he ever considered using the bullet on me. Even after I scared him half to death that first full moon."

"But you could control it," I said. "You didn't kill him."

Harnock snorted. "I tried."

He took a long sip of his coffee and stared at the bookshelf behind my left shoulder. I'd spent enough time at Brigitte's to know what he saw there. Medical textbooks on the top shelf, teaching guides underneath. The shelf in the middle bare, save a framed picture of Brigitte and me during our college days, and beside that, a small wooden cross.

When he spoke, his eyes were far away, lost in memory. "I don't remember much about that first shift except the pain. It's common for new wolves to lose themselves to a blood rage in that first night, attacking anything in sight. We were alone in the wilds, Nathaniel and I, there would have been no one to attack except him. But I awoke the next morning, naked and cold. And he was still there, pulling extra clothes from his pack, passing them to me without a word. He never talked about that night, never told me what I did, but he couldn't hide the scratch marks on his chest, the blood that seeped through his shirt."

Harnock swallowed hard and met my eyes. "He's a good

man. He stayed with me when he didn't need to. It was only when I told him that I was traveling here to be near Artemis again that we parted ways. By then I knew how to control the shift and I didn't lose myself when I changed, it was safe to come to the city."

"Did he tell you why he wouldn't come with you?"

"He said he'd burned too many bridges in this city," Harnock said.

I sipped my coffee in silence. What brought him back here? If it was this dangerous for him in the city, why had he returned?

My phone rang and I jumped. Damn, I was tired.

I checked the caller ID. "Hey, Sammy, what's up?"

"Our vampire friend has cut quite the swath through the underground."

"Hesta?"

Harnock placed his mug on a coaster on the table beside him and disappeared down the hall. Checking on Nathaniel, I assumed.

"Once I had a name, it wasn't too difficult to track her," Samuel said. "Half of my underground contacts had heard of her or worked for her in the last month."

"Busy girl," I said. "Does anyone know where to find her now?"

"No one who would share," Samuel said. "Apparently, she pops up, pulls together a crew, does a job, and disappears again. She's been taking out warehouses and cargo ships all throughout the city."

"Why hasn't NOPD gotten her yet?"

"She doesn't use the same crew more than once," Samuel said. "I don't know how she does it, but she uses a fresh batch of people each time, hangs back herself, stays off the cameras. NOPD might not even realize that all the thefts are connected."

"How do we know it's her?"

"Get this, every mention of her has the same description. Black hair, blue butterfly tattoo, and necklace around her neck with a whopper of a yellow jewel on the end of it. A jewel that looks like it's been lit with fire."

"Sounds like something I'd call a Firestone," I mused. My mind whirred, putting together a plan.

"Is she looking for a new crew?" I asked. "Could she use a strapping young Cajun and brown-haired beauty with PI experience?"

"No dice," Samuel said. I heard the sound of a horn honking behind him, he must have been walking along the street somewhere. A gust of wind distorted the sound. "No one's heard from her in a week. Three weeks of jobs every two days and then nothing. Maybe she's keeping her head down because the city's gotten too hot."

"Yeah, or maybe she's made enough to retire and live like a queen," I said.

"Sounds nice," Samuel said. "Not the queen part but retiring I could do."

"You'd be bored in a week," I pointed out.

Samuel hummed and I listened to the sound of him walking for a moment. A hawker yelled out his wares close to the phone.

"What about *The Thorn?*" I asked. "Did you find out anything about that?"

"Not a clue," Samuel said. "Far as I can tell, no one's heard of it."

"Tell him to look up *Red Rose on the River.*"

I looked up to see Nathaniel standing at the entrance to

the hallway. He wore a black sweater that was much too big on him. He must have borrowed it from Harnock.

"Tell him," Nathaniel insisted.

"*Red Rose on the River*," I said into the phone. "What about that?"

"The riverboat?" Samuel asked. "To my knowledge, it's still operational despite NOPD's best efforts."

"Riverboat," I said, raising an eyebrow at Nathaniel. The pirate staggered forward a step before collapsing into the armchair Harnock had vacated. He should have slept longer. Deep lines carved around the corners of his eyes. He gestured toward the phone.

I put the phone on speaker mode. "Hey Sammy, long story, but you're on speakerphone. Nathaniel's here."

Samuel's voice was flat. "Hi."

Harnock waved as he crossed the room toward the door. I nodded. Now that Nathaniel was awake, I'm sure he wanted to get home to Artemis.

Nathaniel seemed to be catching his breath even from the few steps he took up the hall. He leaned forward so the phone could pick up his speech. "Are you familiar with the riverboat's reputation?"

"It's an illegal casino," Samuel said. "The fae who run it couldn't get a permit to operate within the city, so they took to the water. Less regulation that way."

"That's the one," Nathaniel said. "But it's not just any fae who run it." He took a deep breath and winced. "It's high fae."

Samuel sucked a breath in through his teeth.

High fae were hardly seen in the city. They kept themselves apart from the rest of the non-human citizens, but the human government wouldn't allow them into their ranks. They always struck me as aloof, self-important. But they were powerful mages. I wouldn't want to piss one off, that's for sure.

"Last time I was in the city," Nathaniel continued, "*Red Rose on the River* changed its name at night. After dark, the casino on board became a tad less friendly to the humans it served during the day. Those who frequented it at night called it *The Thorn*."

"We need to make a plan," Samuel said. "Where are you?"

"Brigitte's."

"I'll be right there."

For some reason, having Samuel on the phone had acted as a buffer. Now that we'd hung up, it was just the two of us. Watching each other without outright staring across Brigitte's living room. Neither one quite sure how to begin. Nathaniel's eyes were crystal blue, bright in his tanned face. Aquamarine. Not staring was hard. I could lose myself in them.

"Coffee?" I asked suddenly, startling us both.

"Um, sure," Nathaniel said. He looked down at his hands, flexing his knuckles against the new skin. I hated that his confidence was gone. I hated that he wasn't the same swaggering pirate who had annoyed me over the last few weeks.

I disappeared into the kitchen welcoming the chance to catch my breath, to get my pounding heart under control. What was wrong with me? Why couldn't I just talk to him, crack a joke, ease the tension with some self-deprecating humor? I was good at that. I leaned back against the counter and placed my forehead in my palm. I was stupid, that's why.

"Hey," Nathaniel said.

I jumped and let out an unnatural squeak.

"Sorry," he said. "Honestly, I hate coffee. Can I just have some water maybe?"

I looked at him like he'd grown a second head. "Don't like coffee? What is wrong with you?"

Nathaniel shrugged. "Too many things to count."

I laughed, tension easing. He'd beaten me to the self-deprecating humor.

I poured him a glass from the pitcher beside the sink. Our hands touched as I handed it to him, his skin warm against mine.

"Thank you," he said, our eyes locking.

"Don't mention it," I breathed. I couldn't let go of the glass, frozen in his gaze.

"You came for me," he said softly. I wasn't sure if I misheard. "You saved my life."

I took my hand back. "It's not enough," I said.

A distressed look crossed his face, and I turned away.

There were a few dishes in the sink: a plate, a fork, the mug that Harnock had used. I started washing them, turning the water on warm enough to scald away the feeling of his hand on mine.

"I'm not going to lie," Nathaniel said, leaning against the counter beside the sink, "I still dream about you."

A lump rose in my throat, threatening to choke me.

"Some of the time it's you and me on the ship," he said. "When you—"

He stopped and I squeezed my eyes shut, my hands growing still in the sink.

"But other times, it's not that," he continued. "Sometimes you smile at me. You sing for me in the waves, and I go to you. Not because I have to—"

He drew closer, his hip was beside mine, his voice a whisper in my ear. "But because I want to."

His knuckle was warm against my cheek, wiping away a tear I hadn't realized had fallen.

"When I confronted you on the street, outside the warehouse, I thought it would make me feel better. I thought yelling at you and leaving you behind would take away the anger I had, but it didn't. I had to find that out for myself."

I held my breath. He was too close. His breath soft on my ear, like a kiss.

"I don't hate you for what you did, Meranda," he said. "Some days I wish I did. But I can't. I can't stay away from you. Since I saw you at Baxter's, I've been drawn to you."

I shook my head, not trusting myself to speak without my voice breaking.

"It's not just the ghosts," he said. "It's not just that I needed your powers. It's you. I need to be near you. The thought of being apart—"

"It's my fault," I said, finally turning toward him. He was a blur in front of me, distorted by the liquid in my eyes. "It's the siren's call. It still compels you to me."

"I don't believe that," Nathaniel insisted. He grabbed my hands, his grip strong and sure. I hated to admit how much I wanted those hands on me, touching my skin, wrapping around me.

"It's the truth," I said. "I sang for you and now you can't escape me. You can't help yourself."

"No," Nathaniel said. A tone of desperation entered his words. "That's not it. That can't be it."

"I'm sorry," I said, pushing his hands away. "It's the only

explanation. There's no other way you could look past what I did."

"I forgive you, Meranda."

My heart broke. I gasped out a sob. It wasn't true. It wasn't him speaking. It was my powers compelling him. It had to be.

"Look at me," he said. His voice fierce and urgent. I met his gaze, breath hitching in my throat. "I. Forgive. You."

"You can't," I gasped out.

"Why not?"

"Because I don't forgive me!" I yelled. I gripped the counter beside me to keep from falling to the floor. My breath came in ragged gasps, filling the silence my words had left. The room was spinning.

My ears rang at the words I had said.

"That sounds like a you problem," Nathaniel said. The familiar flippancy was back in his voice.

I snapped my eyes up to him. Centering myself. "What?"

"You heard me," Nathaniel said.

A knock sounded from the front room, but my feet were rooted to the floor.

Nathaniel gave me one last look before leaving the kitchen.

I made it to the living room in time to see Samuel throwing some serious side-eye at my pirate as he walked in. My pirate? What? No.

"Coffee's in the kitchen," I said and took a seat on the couch. My brain was muddled. Hurrying to get back into case-mode after my conversation with Nathaniel.

"I'm fine," Samuel said, taking the far seat on the couch and leaving the armchair for Nathaniel. "First off, if our magical artifacts expert is here anyway, I have a few questions."

Nathaniel lowered himself into the chair, stifling a wince. "Shoot," he said.

"What's a Firestone?"

Nathaniel's eyes lit up. "A Firestone?" he asked. "Is that what you think Poincare lost?"

"Could be," Samuel said, his tone guarded. "Is it something he'd be likely to have smuggled in?"

"A Firestone is worth more than you or I will see in a lifetime." Nathaniel leaned forward in his chair. "It's a combination of volcanic rock and ancient magic. They can only be forged on the island of St. Lucia, very rare, very dangerous.

"You think the arcane protective amulet was bad, a Firestone is far more volatile. It can be keyed to one person. Only one at a time. Anyone else tries to touch it, they'll lose a limb, if not their life."

"What does it do?" I asked.

"It enhances natural abilities. A human could gain advanced strength, speed," Nathaniel said.

"And a vampire—" Samuel trailed off.

An uncomfortable chill crept into my chest. We didn't know. Each vampire came with their own specific abilities. Some could influence with their speech; some could freeze a person with a look. An enhanced vampire could very well be unstoppable.

"No wonder Poincare didn't involve the NOPD," I said. "If he was caught sneaking something like that into the city, it wouldn't matter how many members of the city council he had in his pocket; they couldn't ignore that kind of danger."

It made sense now, why Poincare had hired an investigative agency that was too small to cause real ripples in the city. He couldn't afford the kind of attention a larger agency would bring. He didn't hire us because he believed in us, he hired us because we were in no position to cause trouble based on what we found. Even if we tried to go to the authorities with what we knew, who would believe us? A no-name detective and a disgraced ex-cop.

With his influence in the city, he could control us. A sour taste filled my mouth. We were being used.

"I made some calls on the way," Samuel said. "*Red Rose on the River* is only in town for the next few days. If we want to catch Hesta there, we don't have long."

"Let's go tonight," I said. "We can't be sure that she'll be there this evening, but we can at least scope it out, find out what we're dealing with."

"Correct me if I'm wrong," Nathaniel interjected, "but admission to *The Thorn* is by invitation only."

Samuel nodded. "That's the way I understand it."

"Shit."

"No," Nathaniel said. "It's probably quite nice inside."

I glared at him, but deep down I was glad his humor was back.

"Either way, we'll want to be there when Hesta is," Samuel said. "I don't know about you, but an elite waterbound casino isn't exactly the kind of place I fit in. We may only get one shot at this. There's a gala tomorrow night, if Hesta is in any way close to the descriptions I've heard of her, she wouldn't miss it."

Tomorrow. That only gave us one day to prepare. And

one day after until our deadline with Poincare. If we didn't get his amulet back at that gala, we were royally screwed.

"You know who could probably get us an invite," I said, not meeting Samuel's gaze. Nathaniel threw me a wry grin as though he already knew the answer.

"Don't say it," Samuel growled beside me.

"Oleksandr."

"Dammit."

"Sorry," I said.

"I'm not," Nathaniel said.

Chapter Nineteen

I met Florentina on Brigitte's front porch. A cool breeze chased fallen leaves down the street. The crisp air nipped at my cheeks.

My aunt was the picture of Halloween spirit without even trying. Her wide hooped skirt was draped with dark fabric, black lace poking out around the hem. The bodice was a deep maroon, and the ends of her sleeves trailed to her hips in the same black lace that showed beneath. A dark silk headwrap bound around her hair, hiding all but the ends of it, graying coils sticking out behind her head.

"Samuel tells me you're looking for a Firestone," she said. Her eyes glinted in the setting sun whose rays bathed Brigitte's front porch.

We sat side by side on white painted rocking chairs. A tray holding a lemonade pitcher and two glasses sat between us. A gift for asking Florentina to meet me here on such short notice. I couldn't cook, but lemonade I could do.

"That's how it's looking," I said. "You know much about Firestones?"

Florentina's smile was soft, knowing. She didn't say

anything in answer, but as usual she knew more than she let on.

"I didn't call you here to ask about the case," I said. "Not that case, anyway."

"Ah," Florentina said. "Your ghosts."

"Not my ghosts," I said. I stirred a long spoon in my glass, watching the ice and lemon slices chase each other in a circle. "Nathaniel's ghosts."

"Nathaniel's ghosts," Florentina repeated, her gaze far away.

"I couldn't touch them," I said. "It wasn't like when we've practiced with Marie. They weren't just muffled and out of reach. When I wrapped my power around them, they slipped through my grasp. And my head exploded. Like the worst migraine in the world."

"They're not your ghosts," Florentina said as though that should be obvious.

"No, I know," I said. "They're Nathaniel's ghosts. But I couldn't command them. My powers wouldn't work on them."

Florentina tapped her spoon on the rim of her glass. The sound ringing out like a death knell with each word. "Not. Your. Ghosts."

I paused. "They belong to the sea," I said finally.

Florentina raised her glass, a smile widening across her face. "There you have it."

"How do I get them to go back to the sea, then?"

Florentina raised her spoon again. "Not. Your—"

"No, I know. I know. Hang on," I said. Florentina fell silent as I thought. I hated how much this felt like an exam I hadn't studied for.

Not my ghosts. Whose ghosts were they? They haunted

Nathaniel, but they belonged to the sea. Who was supposed to control them in the sea?

I wracked my brain for an inkling of what I needed. I'd heard the lessons of drowned sailors before. Years ago, in the Gulf, we'd all been taught what happened when a sailor drowns. One of the melusines I trained with had asked if they could possess us, if their spirits could take vengeance on the melusine who killed them by taking over their body. The instructor had laughed, sharp teeth bright in the rays of sunlight that moved through the water. A proverb he'd told.

"A captain always goes down with his ship," I said, almost a whisper.

"She remembers," Florentina said. "Thank the universe."

"Their captain should have guided them to the next life. It's his job on the open water to shepherd the souls of his crew. He's the one who gives them peace. Without him going down with the boat, they are stuck here. A haunting."

Florentina nodded along, her eyebrows raised, encouraging me to keep going.

"But their captain was with them," I said. "He was giving them orders, commanding them to attack. To get Nathaniel."

"What exactly did he command them to do?" Florentina was patient as a schoolmaster guiding a student through lessons.

I closed my eyes and thought back. The memories of the attack were a jumble. I couldn't make them out. But that moment. Right before I found that my powers didn't work against them, the captain had said something important.

My eyes snapped open. "Get Nathaniel and get back to the wraith."

I furrowed my brow. "No, not the wraith. The *Wraith*."

I stood so quickly I almost tipped the chair over backward. "Can you wait here?" I asked, zipping up my jacket. "I have to check on something, I won't be long. I can't leave Nathaniel inside unprotected, not if his ghosts come back."

Florentina nodded once as though she had expected me to ask her. She sat back in her chair, rocking softly back and forth as she sipped from her lemonade.

I tore down the front walk and up the street.

I had to find a streetcar. There were questions that needed answers.

The museum's lights were out. They closed their doors early on weekdays. Their main demographic being school trips, they practically lost money on the electricity alone if they kept the building open past 5pm. I crept along the side of the building, hoping I could remember which door had a broken alarm.

My shoulders tensed as I jimmied the lock, expecting blaring sirens and spotlights at any moment. The evening remained quiet. I pushed the door open and tiptoed into the museum lobby.

The lobby floor was empty, shining in the streetlights that came in the front windows. They must have just washed them. The werewolf skeleton on display presided over the scene. Sharp teeth standing out in the low light. Its grin garish and sad in the emptiness of the museum.

I stepped carefully across the floor, making my way toward the featured display. I couldn't believe it had only been a week since I'd first seen it. The heavy red drapes were tied up off the floor, making way for the cleaners I assumed. I stayed close to the wall to keep from leaving a trail of footprints across the laminate.

My breath caught in my throat as I saw the ship again. When I'd first seen it, the room had been full of distractions. Sounds and smells piped in, small children milling about, spotlights drawing the eye to specific points. Now, without all those, *Sea Wraith* stood out in its quiet simplicity. The wood of its hull was a dark oak, powerful and strong. The masts had to be some kind of pine, only a slightly lighter shade than the deck beneath. The figurehead maintained her downcast gaze, the feeling of loss somehow even more powerful in the empty room.

I sat cross-legged on the floor before the carved melusine. Hands on my knees, shoulders relaxed. I reached toward the ship with my powers. *Talk to me,* I thought. *What happened to you?*

A presence sparked before me, vague, like seeing something out of the corner of your eye. I focused my powers on it, wrapping around it, feeling its shape. Concentrating my power in that one place, I deafened to the rest of the world. The extra focus brought the spirit into view in my mind's eye.

Her hair was long and wavy, it undulated before me as though she was under water. Her bare chest and stomach were tanned, muscles flexing as she too moved like she was treading in the ocean. Blue-green tail flicked to and fro, working with her arms as though to maintain position in a current. She would have looked like a true melusine if it weren't for her eyes, all white sclera, no iris or pupil.

"*Sea Wraith*," I called her.

The white eyes focused on me, as though seeing me for the first time. Her mouth opened and closed, no sound coming out.

"You are not at peace," I said, putting a name to what

she felt. "The spirit of a ship should be at rest once its work is complete."

The wraith grew still as though only just realizing she didn't have to tread water. "Why am I not?" she asked, her voice a soft whisper.

My hold on her was tenuous. A ship's spirit wasn't what I had been created to control. She was more slippery than the sailors I had been unable to grasp earlier that day.

"Where is your captain?"

A distressed look came across her face, her eyes pinched, narrowing the white to near slits. A noise like the creaking of wood came from her throat.

I kept my tone gentle, afraid to scare the spirit back into her ship. "Who is your captain?"

The spirit's eyes snapped open; her mouth widened to almost twice its size. I winced as the sound of shrieking wood filled the room. The image of splintering masts filled my mind, water rushing into holds, a hull breached.

I sank an ounce of my power into my voice. "*Who is your captain?*"

"I don't know!" the spirit shrieked. My hold on her slipped and she vanished.

I opened my eyes to see the six sailors from earlier standing before me. Half of them swung heavy chains from their hands, one hoisted a harpoon gun, two more brandished swords. I scrambled to my feet.

"Stay back," I warned, not really sure how I could even enforce such a demand.

The captain materialized before me. This close, I could see the pockmarks on his face, smell the foulness of his breath like rancid meat.

"Well, well, well," he said. "Twice in one day can't be coincidence. You must be looking for trouble."

"Oh, is this your ship?" I asked. "Funny, her spirit doesn't recognize you."

If I could distract them long enough, maybe confuse them enough, I could bolt for the exit. If my suspicions were correct, big fat if, then they wouldn't be able to travel far from their ship. If I could put enough distance between me and the *Wraith*, I'd be safe.

The captain's teeth gnashed at me, a clatter of sound. "She's confused from the wreck."

The sailors behind him were beginning to eye each other. Without clear orders to attack, they were losing their momentum. They may not even maintain their hold of this plane if I kept them unsure.

"Or maybe," I said, leaning close, not a hint of fear in my tone despite the chill in my gut, "You're not the real captain. Which leads me to ask," I nodded my head toward the sailors behind him, "Why are they following you?"

Four sailors disappeared from the room. I fixed my eyes on the ghost before me. "Dissension in the ranks," I tsked. "But I'm guessing that's nothing foreign to you."

My mind was grasping onto the possible explanations for what I had seen. It wasn't the entire ship's crew that was tied to this life, only a few. The ship's testimony alone was evidence enough for what had occurred before she went down. The fact that they were also tied to Nathaniel... well, that could only mean one thing.

"Mutiny," I hissed. The two sailors left flickered.

"Capital crimes on the high seas," I said. "You must have convinced most of the crew to follow you for them to have passed on when you drowned. What must it have felt like when you couldn't gain rest for yourself?"

The would-be captain let out a gurgling sound, deep in his throat as I reminded him of his death. He coughed up sea water, spilling it across the exhibit floor. A crab scuttled from the corner of his mouth and ran up his cheek.

"I was the captain," he said. "The ship was under my command."

"You don't believe that," I said. "If you did, you would have found peace with the others who believed in you. As it is, you are stuck here, stranded until your true captain can guide you to the great beyond. Shepherdless. Cursed to wander for your disloyalty. And these sorry souls, trusting in their true captain, are cursed to wander with you. Because Nathaniel wasn't even on that ship when it went down, was he?" I asked. I stepped forward and all three ghosts before me cowered back a step, losing confidence as I spoke. "You'd already thrown him off the ship like damn cowards."

The last two sailors disappeared, either forced from this plane or retreating on their own, I didn't care which.

The mutinous spirit flickered, his anger flashing across his face. "*He* was the coward," he bellowed. A chain was in his hand suddenly, its heavy links clanking against each other as he rattled it toward me. "Nathaniel was still on that ship. He abandoned us in our hour of greatest need. He should have been there for us, but he left!" Sea water sprayed from his mouth, splattering across my face. I resisted the urge to flinch.

"We're here to correct a wrong," the ghost said. "We will undo Nathaniel's mistake. And when he is dead, he will lead us on. We will have peace." The chain rattled once more, a ghostly weapon gaining physical form. "The only problem is you, standing in our way."

I ducked as the chain sailed toward my head, anticipating the attack. I cursed myself for having stripped the iron knuckles off my hands earlier that day and leaving them in Harnock's truck. I dodged to the left as the chain came crashing down where I had been standing a moment before. Shit. He was going to kill me. This ghost I couldn't touch was going to kill me and then he was going to kill Nathaniel.

I cast my eyes around the room, looking for a weapon. Metal stands held a velvet rope that must have cordoned off the exhibit before they opened. From the looks of them, they were steel, not iron. Useless to me.

The ghost pivoted and let out a growl, sending the chain flying my direction once more. I leapt to the side and rolled behind the ship, disappearing from his view for a brief moment. I could hear him reeling the chain back in. There wasn't much time before he came around the corner, I had to move. I had to do something.

"They say drowning is the most painful way to die," I called out. I heard a grunt as my words impacted his being. "They say by the end your lungs are desperate for air, your brain screaming for oxygen. That you welcome death long before it finally takes you."

A cough sounded on the other side of the ship. A gagging sound and another splatter of sea water. It was working. I caught sight of a flash of light behind a heavy black curtain in the back of the room. An exit sign. Hell yes.

I didn't have long before he got his control back. "Your cells literally explode," I said. "The sea water lysing through them until they burst, every blood vessel blowing at once and staining your eyes red."

The man who came around the corner was a demon. His body had transformed as I spoke, remembering its death. I let out a yell of pain as the chain lashed my leg. It felt as though my bone shattered beneath its weight. He was atop me then, straddling my hips. The stench of his breath in my face, vomit and sea water. His nose was missing, eaten by whatever fish had gotten to his body after it descended beneath the waves. And there were those red eyes, bright as the exit sign I couldn't reach.

I brought my arms up to protect my face and cried out as the chain smashed into my elbows. He wasn't attacking my face, he had the chain pressed against my throat, leaning on it with all his might. He was going to choke me to death.

Images of Peter Grassi floated before my vision. The cabin on the shores of Manchac. It was happening again. No, no, no. My vision blurred, dark spots dancing before my eyes. I brought my arms down on his elbows, trying to break through the lock he had on them. My fists passed right through him as he turned his arms to static. I was able to take a quick half breath before he reformed, and the pressure was back.

Shit. How was he so good at that?

I bucked my hips, trying to dislodge him, knock him off balance, but all his weight was against my throat, crushing my trachea. Sea water rained down on my face, spewing from the ghost's mouth. Even if I could take another breath, I'd drown in the deluge.

I was going to die. I was going to die alone, and no one would know where I was. The museum staff would find my body in the morning. A small brunette in a puddle of ocean water, I could see the headlines now. The lack of oxygen was making me delirious.

This was it, the puddle forming around me would be as close as I'd get to my ocean home. My head pounded; my vision narrowed.

"Get off of her."

The command came from the doorway to the exhibit. I almost couldn't make it out over the ringing in my ears, but the pressure left my chest. The chain slid from my throat, and I twisted to the side coughing.

"You," the ghostly demand came, nearly a hiss.

"Yeah, me," my rescuer said. "Back away from her, Tanner."

I could make out the ghostly boots as they stepped back. My vision cleared enough to see who was approaching closer. Nathaniel?

A grumble sounded from Tanner.

"Shut it," Nathaniel commanded. I could almost feel the power coming off him, a wave of it crashing through the room. "Now, forgive me if I'm a bit out of practice giving orders. It has been years since you took my ship from me. So there's no room for ambiguity, I will say this once. Begone!"

Tanner let out a guttural yell and vanished.

Nathaniel dropped to my side. "Can you stand?"

My voice sounded like a tortured toad. "I don't know. My leg."

He placed a hand on my shin, and I sucked in a breath. That stung.

I noticed too late, my phone, slipped out of my back pocket and unresponsive in the puddle the ghost had left. I pressed the buttons on either side of the screen with no change. Only my reflection staring back at me from the black surface. I made a grumbling noise and shoved it into my back pocket, holding my left leg out straight so I wouldn't put pressure on the injury.

"Hold still," Nathaniel said.

"What are you—"

He scooped me up in his arms, much the way Harnock had earlier that day, but with far less surety. I let out a squawk as we tipped sideways.

"I said hold still," he said.

I froze. I had to trust him not to drop me. Ugh, I hated that so much.

He carried me back through the front room of the museum.

I tried to move my ankle and winced as pain lanced up my leg. "Please tell me you have a car."

"Grab my phone," he said. "Back pocket."

I reached into the pocket of his jeans, trying to ignore how firm his muscles were underneath the fabric.

"I'll call Samuel," I said. "He can bring the Agency car over. I can't believe you came. You saved my life."

Nathaniel didn't reply.

I pressed the phone to my ear, listening to it ring.

"Dammit," I said, half to myself. "You know what this means?"

"What?"

"We're not even anymore."

I looked up at his face, but he kept his eyes pointed front. "I wasn't counting."

Chapter Twenty

Samuel gave me a proper chastising when he showed up. How could I leave him in the house and sneak off to confront ghosts on my own? How could I not tell him where I was going? Didn't I know I could have died?

I made the appropriate agreements and apologies all while gesturing to my injured leg and putting on my best attempt at puppy dog eyes. Finally, he fell silent, content to glower at me in the rearview mirror.

Nathaniel had placed me in the back seat, careful to guide my legs in without jostling them too much. The ache had faded to a dull throbbing, but the swelling had brought my calf to nearly twice its normal circumference. Also, my toes were growing numb. That couldn't be a good sign.

We sped toward Brigitte's house as fast as local speed limits would allow. I gritted my teeth and tried not to believe that Sammy was hitting every pothole in the road on purpose. Nathaniel for his part remained silent, unmoving in the passenger seat beside my partner. For once, they agreed on something. They were both pissed at me.

"I have to call Oleksandr," I said. "We're cutting it close for invitations as it is, we have to get him on it now."

"That would have been a good idea *before* you ran off to get yourself killed," Samuel said, his eyes on me in the mirror again.

"Ouch my leg," I said, plaintively.

Nathaniel snorted but passed his phone back to me.

"I don't like this," Samuel said. His knuckles whitening on the steering wheel.

"Oleksandr's not so bad," Nathaniel offered. "Once you get to know him."

I dialed the number. Please pick up, please pick up.

"Nathaniel?" Oleksandr's voice hit my ears like a cool stream washing over my soul. Smooth, chilling.

"No, it's Meranda."

"You have Nathaniel's phone," Oleksandr purred. "Interesting."

I ignored his intimation. "Have you been to *The Thorn* recently?"

"Have I—" Oleksandr paused as though thinking through the possible reasons I would be asking. "You need an invite," he said finally.

"Three actually," I said. "For tomorrow. Can you make it happen?"

"The fae won't be happy if you bring humans onto their boat," Oleksandr warned. I could hear a tapping of a keyboard somewhere near the phone.

"They don't have to know," I said.

"Oh, they'll know," Oleksandr assured me.

"Well, hopefully they'll give us a chance before kicking us out."

The silence stretched longer than I liked. A few more keystrokes sounded, rapid fire, practiced.

"It's done," he said. "It wouldn't be the first time I brought someone they didn't approve of."

"You're coming too?" I asked.

"*The Thorn's* last night in New Orleans for the season? I've had it in my calendar for weeks. I'll drop your invitations off at the Agency tomorrow afternoon. Please tell me you have something suitable to wear."

"I think I have a dress made of gray and wool," I offered.

A distressed noise sounded from the other end of the line. "Don't you dare. I'll bring something with me. And don't think you've gotten out of an explanation. I want to hear everything when I stop by tomorrow."

The line went dead, and I looked up to two pairs of eyes on me.

"We're in," I said, trying my hand at an encouraging smile.

"The bloodsucker's coming too?" Samuel asked.

I gave him a half shrug. "He got us in, didn't he?"

"You probably shouldn't call him that when we're working with him," Nathaniel said. "He has more patience than I've seen in any other vampire, but I'm sure it has its limits."

Samuel growled, but I caught a glimpse of Nathaniel's face in the side mirror. He was smiling.

Samuel, Oleksandr, and Nathaniel all stuck on a riverboat at night? It was the premise to a joke. Or a really, really bloody tragedy. Either way, it was sure to be entertaining.

I settled back against the seats and closed my eyes.

Even if Hesta was at the gala, we still needed a plan to get the Firestone from her. And a good night's sleep. We could all use a good night's sleep.

I let out a hiss as we jostled over another pothole.

Dammit.

Brigitte, it seemed, had not slept well. As soon as we walked through the door, well, limped in my case, she smacked a hand against Samuel's shoulder.

"What did you let her do?" she demanded.

"Ow, it wasn't me," Samuel protested. "She snuck out without telling anyone."

"You what?" Brigitte whirled to me. I shrank back as far as I could while still being supported by Samuel's arm.

"Twice in one day, Meranda," she exclaimed. "You come to me injured twice in one day?!"

"Don't yell at me," I protested. "I have an owie."

The puppy dog eyes were far less effective against the healer. "Just sit on the couch and don't move. Don't move a muscle." She stomped down the hall and Samuel dumped me unceremoniously onto the couch.

Ow, I mouthed at him.

He shrugged and walked into the kitchen. Nathaniel dropped into the armchair beside the bookcase and pulled a magazine off the shelf. *Cleaning and Organizing the House-wife Way*. He made a face and put it back.

"I'm sorry," I said as Brigitte stalked back into the living room.

"Don't talk," Brigitte said. "I'm not happy with you right now and it's much harder to heal someone when you're pissed at them."

I sat back and made a lip zipping motion, tossing the key over my shoulder like we used to do as children.

Brigitte didn't look amused. "I go to take a simple nap, everyone is healed. You're healed. And when I wake up, you're stumbling through my door with—" she ran a hand over my pant leg, a quick scan, "—a sprained ankle."

"Sprained?" I asked. "No, I'm sure it's broken. It hurt like a m—"

Brigitte shot me a glare that threatened death.

"—uffin top?"

"I'm covering you with bubble wrap," she said. "Please, tell me you'll stay off this for the next few days. I can just bind it and move on?"

"You're very pretty."

Brigitte brought her fingers to her temples and cast a glance toward the cross on the middle bookshelf. Praying for patience, I was sure.

"We finally found a way to get Poincare's amulet back," I said. "If all goes well, we'll have it in hand tomorrow night. It's just one more night and we're done."

Brigitte fixed her eyes on me, the hazel glowing fiercely in the light cast from the lamp in the corner. "I'm tired," she said. "I am out of practice and exhausted. I haven't had to heal this many bodies at once since my days studying in Atlanta. It makes me feel guilty that I can't do more, but I'm so tired I feel like I could sleep for a week. The reserves are harder to fill here, there's less to draw upon in this city. Too much darkness in these streets."

I nodded along, but I didn't really understand the specifics. I knew her powers were like a well and it took time for her to replenish them in between drawing from it, but I didn't know of many ways to refill her other than time.

"If you come back tomorrow, on the brink of death," she choked once and shook her head. "I don't know if I'll be able to help."

"I'll be careful," I said. "I promise."

She'd told me once that good feelings helped. Buildings that held joy and hope could fill her reserves. Bring her back up. This city had too few of those that weren't also tainted with sorrow and death. Purely joy-filled places were a rarity. Sometimes as we waited for her to re-fill, we curled up on the couch and watched sappy movies. They seemed to help even if she cried the whole way through them. I didn't understand it.

I looked down at my ankle, the swelling above it. "If you can't fix my leg, it's fine. I'll find a way—"

"Don't," Brigitte said. "You can barely walk. We wait much longer, and we'll have to amputate your toes."

I was sure the look on my face conveyed the horror I felt.

Brigitte laughed. "Okay, now I feel better."

I crossed my arms over my chest and pretended to pout but failed miserably.

"Hold still," Brigitte said.

"Yes, ma'am," I said. "And when this is all over, we're having a movie night. Your pick."

Brigitte raised her hands, bringing the glow close to her face as she took a deep breath. "Chick flicks, it is."

I swallowed the urge to protest.

"Chick flicks, it is."

"Chick flicks, it is," Nathaniel said from his chair.

We both startled slightly. We'd forgotten he was even there. Brigitte shrugged.

If we all survived tomorrow, I guess Nathaniel was invited to movie night.

Chapter Twenty-One

Oleksandr arrived at the Agency at eight the next morning. I hadn't expected him to be so early, and we were both surprised to find me in a black V-neck, lounge pants, and soft slippers.

"You're not dressed." Oleksandr raised an eyebrow at the bunny ears sticking up from the slipper's toes.

"You're early." I turned and left him at the doorway, making my way up the hall.

"I never gave you a time," he called after me.

"Boys are in Dad's office," I called back. "Coffee?"

"Only if there's cream."

I loaded up a tray from the kitchen with a thermos of hot coffee and a porcelain pitcher of cream. There were only three matching clean mugs, so I dropped those on the tray and tucked a reusable to-go cup under my chin.

I toed open the door to Dad's office to find a stiff silence had settled on the room since I'd left. Oleksandr patted the thick briefcase that he carried, holding it before him almost like a shield. Samuel glowered at him from across the room behind Dad's desk. Nathaniel leaned back on the couch, arms tucked behind his head, watching the two with an amused glimmer in his eyes.

"Coffee's hot." I interrupted whatever staring contest was occurring, stepping between Oleksandr and the desk. I dumped the tray into Nathaniel's arms. He wasn't doing anything useful anyway. "Come and get it."

I pulled a folding table from where Dad usually stored it behind the bookshelf. It was only a card table, not taking up too much space on the floor, but with three other bodies in there, the room was increasingly shrinking.

Samuel poured his coffee and retreated back behind the desk.

"What's so important about *The Thorn?*" Oleksandr asked.

I perched on the arm of the couch. "You remember taking me to talk to the pixie who lost some of Poincare's cargo?"

Oleksandr inclined his head ever so slightly.

"We found what he's missing," I said. "It's a Firestone, taken by some vampire out of Clan Montrose. She goes by Hesta."

An eyebrow quirked up on Oleksandr's face. "Clan Montrose, you say? It's not often I see a vampire running loose out of their halls. Let alone, stealing a Firestone from a local businessman."

"She didn't stop with the amulet," I said. "She's been stealing from individuals and businesses up and down the Mississippi since she got her hands on the stone. Like she's got some kind of high from it."

"Sounds like a regular menace," Oleksandr's tone was thoughtful, slow.

"None of her crews can tell us much about her," Samuel said. "She gets a different set each time, but somehow, she's extremely forgettable once they're done with the job. Must be paying them a pretty penny to keep their mouths shut."

"I wouldn't be so sure," Oleksandr said. "Clan Montrose is full of mentats. Not every vampire out of there, but many of them. I don't know Hesta specifically, but it wouldn't surprise me if she had a knack for helping people forget."

"And with a Firestone..." I pressed the cup against my chin as I considered the possibilities. Just how powerful would she be? We needed a more firm plan.

I gestured Oleksandr toward the table. "You have the invitations?"

"Even better." He set the briefcase on the table and popped the latches with a snap. "I have schematics."

"I'm a sucker for a good blueprint," I murmured, leaning forward.

Oleksandr spread out a thin paper sketched with pencil. A skeleton of a riverboat stared back at me labels written along the edges with arrows pointing to their corresponding parts.

"*Red Rose on the River* is a three-story riverboat." Oleksandr ran his hand over the paper. "It was purchased by the high fae five years ago, shortly after they moved out of the city."

Samuel piped up from his place behind Dad's computer. "The fae were nothing but trouble to the city council when they first arrived, buying up businesses along the waterfront, threatening other local owners to get them to sell."

"Like a mafia?" I asked.

"Exactly like a mafia," Oleksandr said. He poured some cream into his mug, setting the pitcher back onto the tray on Nathaniel's lap with a clatter. "There was one skirmish with law enforcement, right as they were getting started. With fae magic, though—let's just say, it didn't end well for the humans."

I breathed in the strong scent of my coffee, warmth spreading across my face from the steam. I couldn't imagine the blood that must have been spilled at that encounter. Dad had talked about it, even he had looked sick as he described it.

"Neither side wanted a repeat of that event," Oleksandr continued. "The NOPD turned a blind eye for a few months as the fae seemed to stop their expanding empire. The City Council hoped the problem had resolved itself, that the fae were content with their section of warehouses and buildings along the Mississippi as the vampire clans were happy to stay within their compounds."

"But the fae aren't like vampires at all," Nathaniel said from the couch, his eyes unfocused on the carpet before him.

I searched his face from across the room, wondering what he'd seen of the high fae. I'd never interacted with them, only their lesser counterparts.

"It was one more offense that set the humans off," Oleksandr said. "One business owner complaining that he had been threatened. That was all the City Council needed to retaliate. They weren't going to take a chance meeting the fae on equal ground again."

All three men remained silent for a moment. They all knew what had happened. I, too, had walked past those burned-out buildings on the river walk. The fences of iron that crossed entrances, preventing the fair folk from ever returning to claim their businesses.

"Petros took his people and left," Oleksandr said. "He sent most of them away, the city too small for them to live among the humans safely. He and a few of his court remained, buying the riverboat, and taking to the water, out of reach of the City Council and their laws."

"And any chance of a surprise attack," I said.

Oleksandr raised his mug toward me in silent agreement.

"Petros hates the humans now," Oleksandr said. "But he's more than happy to bring them aboard his boat during the day, take their money from them in games of greed and debauchery. There are plenty of willing participants at those tables. And tonight, we'll be there with them."

I shook myself. Oleksandr tapped a finger on the sketch. "The bottom deck holds the main gaming tables. It's easy enough to find a seat at any table there. Anyone with an invitation can buy drinks, gamble their money, order entertainment, what have you."

He slid his finger up to the top deck. "Up here are the exclusive tables. Not only do you need an invitation to the riverboat, but an extension of personal favor from one of Petros' court. That's where Hesta will be. When we get on board, I will send word up. I'm confident I can get us a place."

"Even though we're human?" Nathaniel asked from the couch.

Oleksandr's eyes lingered on me longer than I liked. "Even though you're human. They'll find it—" he searched for the right word. "Entertaining."

I rolled my eyes.

"What's on the second deck?" Samuel came around from behind the desk and stood beside the sketch. He tapped on the paper in between the lower and upper decks. "What does the fae keep here?"

Oleksandr's eyes glittered dark for a moment. "The menagerie."

I ran a hand down the side of the silk dress. It stopped far too soon, too high on my hip. What had Oleksandr been thinking? I glared at the mirror. I knew exactly what he'd been thinking. That it would match the black silk suit he wore and not the two gray ones he'd brought for Nathaniel and Sammy.

Even in the harsh fluorescent lights of the Agency bathroom, the sapphire complimented my olive skin. The bright silk rose to cover one shoulder in a wide rectangle, hiding all of one collarbone but leaving the rest of my neck and shoulders exposed. The waist was tight, form fitted. For guessing at my size, Oleksandr had been spot on. The skirt fabric swooped up to my hip, meeting where the slit began and cascading down to pool in a modest train behind me.

Brigitte let out a whoosh of breath behind me and set the curling iron on the sink counter.

"I wish you had called me earlier," she said. She sprayed down the last section of curls with a sealant. "I didn't have to spend so much time in the lab."

"You had your experiments to attend to," I said. "My hair could wait."

Brigitte put her wrist before my face. Her watch told me I was wrong.

Not that we could really be late, the gala was an all-night event, but I was sure the boys wanted to leave sooner than I could be ready. Meranda and the boys; ugh, we sounded like a crappy band. Or a really, really dirty novel title.

I finished a swoop of eyeliner, praying the second would match. Brigitte took the dark pencil from my hand. "Close your eyes."

I bent my knees so she could reach my face easier and obeyed. My fingers fiddled with the clasp on the diamond bracelet Oleksandr had given me, trying to close it by feel alone. By the time I was finished, Brigitte was done.

"Thanks," I said. I placed my feet into the silver high heels that Oleksandr had insisted on. There were diamonds along the straps to match the bracelet on my wrist. "How'd your experiment go? Did you get the results you expected?"

Brigitte dabbed a pouf of setting powder on my nose before answering. "Not exactly."

"Was it Harnock?" I asked, the unanswered questions finally getting to me. "Was the sample from him?"

"No, it wasn't Harnock." A slight smile touched the edge of Brigitte's mouth. "And it's far more fun to not tell you, so don't expect an answer tonight."

"If I come back in one piece?" I finished threading the buckles around my ankles and stood up straight. I towered over Brigitte.

"You come back in one piece whether I promise to tell you or not," Brigitte said.

"Okay, mom."

"Stop that," Brigitte said, but I could see the smile in her eyes.

We joined the rest of the crew in Dad's office. I managed not to fall on my way down the narrow hallway from the bathroom, but there were a few close calls. I wasn't used to heels this high.

Nathaniel gave out a low whistle as we walked into the room. His gray suit stretched across his shoulders and tapered to his trim waist. Dark shiny shoes peeked out below the gray slacks. His blond hair was tousled slightly, as though he had run his hands through it while it was drying and hadn't bothered to brush it again.

Samuel turned from the computer desk, wearing a matching gray suit, and raised his eyebrows at me. "You clean up nice."

I tried to hide the blush that threatened my cheeks. "Thanks."

Oleksandr held his arm out and I slid my hand onto his cool forearm. "Car's waiting. Shall we?"

I nodded and he guided me back out of the office.

Samuel ducked a head into his grandmother's parlor as we left, calling out a goodbye.

A sleek black limousine waited in front of the Agency. It was probably the nicest car this street had ever seen. Oleksandr waved the other two in before us and then helped me up.

I knew I wouldn't feel comfortable at *The Thorn*. I knew the riverboat and its clientele went through more money in one night than I would see in a year. This wasn't the kind of night I could get used to. I looked around the back of the limo. Samuel picked a stray thread off his sleeve and waved off the offer of champagne Nathaniel made.

Whatever was coming this evening, one thing was sure.

We were dressed for it.

Chapter Twenty-Two

Red Rose on the River was far more impressive in person than Oleksandr's sketch could convey. A massive paddlewheel, painted olive green, sat silent and still at its stern. The boat was painted a bright white that had either been touched up recently or was maintained by magic. Not a touch of gray or dirt marred its surface. Its name stood out in red near the stern and beside it a scarlet rose outlined in black.

A live band played on the first deck, trumpet punctuating the melody of a saxophone. A few whoops and hollers could be heard as attendees clapped along. Two smokestacks rose above the river, towering like giants. Instead of billowing smoke polluting the air, gentle puffs of blue and green emerged. A festive addition to the loud celebration going on below.

The second and third decks seemed quiet compared to the lively scene just above the waterline. I couldn't help my eyes glancing toward that second deck. The quiet coming from it was dark with foreboding. I couldn't get Oleksandr's tone out of my head as he'd told me what was there. *The Menagerie.* I suppressed the urge to shudder.

This close to the Gulf, the urge to dive into the waters and swim away from this place hit strong. The smell of the ocean caressing my senses, beckoning me near. Instinctively, I felt toward the water, sensing what may lie beneath the surface. I was so close. It would be easy to dive in. I shook myself. No, not now. Later.

A gangplank led down to a wooden dock, and I kept hold of Oleksandr's arm until I could grasp its red metal railing. I held the sapphire skirt in one hand as we proceeded up the gangplank.

"Big wheel," Samuel observed.

"If you start singing 'Proud Mary'," Nathaniel said, "they'll find your body in the river."

I shot them both a look over my shoulder, warning them to stop bickering. They fell silent.

Oleksandr flashed our invitations to the two men dressed in white who guarded the top of the walkway. No, not men. Their pointed ears and slightly blue skin belied the truth. Lesser fae.

I took the opportunity to look around the deck as Oleksandr guided me around them. The first deck was open. In between the poles that held up the deck above, rolling doors had been raised, allowing the cool night breeze and sounds of the river to pass though. The floor was filled with tables that held spinning wheels and games for cards or dice. An exclamation of victory rose on my right accompanied soon after by the sounds of celebration.

A bar stood near the stern and lesser fae and pixies wearing buttoned up white uniforms carried drinks and empty glasses about the floor on trays held high above their head.

Oleksandr waved a waiter over and whispered into his ear. The green skinned man flashed pointy teeth and nodded as Oleksandr passed him a folded bill. It vanished into the pixie's shirt, and he disappeared into the crowd.

"I'm getting us a seat at a table up top." Oleksandr answered my questioning look. "In the meantime, let's act like we belong here."

"What are they playing upstairs?"

Oleksandr's cool hand cupped my elbow, he steered me toward an empty seat at a card table. "How are you at blackjack?"

"Crap," I said. "What's up there?"

A fang showed in the corner of Olksandr's smile. "Blackjack."

I matched his smile and hoped my eyes shot daggers as I lowered myself into the empty seat.

"Blackjack's the game, twenty-one is what you're looking for," the dealer said, a practiced spiel. Two cards landed in front of me, I peeked at them. A jack and a six.

Bets went into the center of the table, Oleksandr flicking a ten-dollar bill in for me. He hadn't even seen my cards.

"Stand or hit," the dealer called. "Stand or hit."

"Hit." The man beside me let out a smoker's cough, his stomach jerking with the violence of it. I leaned away from him instinctively and Oleksandr set a hand on my bare shoulder, steadying me.

It was my turn. I hated this game with a burning passion. I'd tried my hand at it once when the school put on a casino night for a fundraiser. Even Brigitte had been better than I. I'd lost every fake chip they had given me at the door. I surely would have lost whatever funds we'd raised if those were on the line.

The dealer was looking at me.

"Hit," I said, hoping my voice sounded confident.

Another card landed in front of me. A seven. Dammit. I flipped the cards over and rose.

"Told you I was crap," I said.

"It's not about winning," Oleksandr murmured, his breath cool against the shell of my ear. "It's about looking like we belong here. They'll let us up top when they're ready, but I'm sure they're watching us now." He glanced over my shoulder. "They're suspicious of the humans."

I turned back toward the table to find Nathaniel in my seat. A new round started, and two cards flew to each player. Nathaniel played with the confidence of someone who knew their craft. Two rounds passed with him doubling the money Oleksandr put up for him before a green tinged pixie glided forward and exchanged his cash for chips.

"Excuse me," Oleksandr said, his hand trailing along my hip. "There's someone over there I must speak to."

I tried not to shudder as his hand left my side. The icy sensation leaving goosebumps in its wake. He was toying with me. Payment for getting our invitations. I wondered how far he would go.

Samuel was at my side, drink in hand, eyes on Nathaniel. "He's good," he said.

"He's amazing," I breathed.

Samuel placed a martini glass in my hand. A lemon twist floated on the surface of the clear liquor. I leaned against his shoulder, but kept my eyes fixed on Nathaniel. "I don't know what Oleksandr is playing at, but I don't trust that it's our game. Once we get upstairs, we find whatever table Hesta is at. Nathaniel's playing. As soon as she's distracted by the game, you nab the Firestone."

"That easy?" Samuel asked.

"It will be around her neck, I'd imagine," I said. "Can't be too hard."

I hadn't told Oleksandr this part of the plan. He didn't need to know what Samuel could do. That magic couldn't touch him. In all the commotion, I hoped our vampire friend wouldn't ask too many questions about *how* Samuel had picked the stone up.

"Any clue how to get off the boat before a pissed off vampire takes us down?"

"How fast can you run?"

A horn sounded from somewhere above us. I cast a questioning look across the floor at Oleksandr, but he just smiled and raised a bloody Mary toward me. I crashed into Samuel as the riverboat jerked forward. Samuel's arms came around me, strong and sure, holding me upright. The sound of water falling came from behind us as the wheel turned, moving us through the river.

"New plan," I said, pushing off him and smoothing the front of the gown. "Once you have your hands on the Firestone, you jump off the deck. I'll be right behind you."

Samuel raised an eyebrow. "And we just leave Nathaniel and Oleksandr behind?"

"Nathaniel should have enough sense to jump in after us," I said.

"Okay, but if it doesn't go as planned," Samuel said, "I'm blaming you."

"I wouldn't expect any less," I said.

A cold presence at my back, Oleksandr's soft voice in my ear. "They're ready for us upstairs."

I stepped forward and place a hand on Nathaniel's shoulder. He brought his warm palm up and cupped it over mine. It was such a natural reaction. So familiar, I wanted to stay that way for a moment. He looked up, his blue eyes glowing with excitement.

"Time to go," I said.

He nodded and folded his hand to the sound of groans from around the table. Distress at their lucky charm moving away, I was sure. A lesser fae gathered Nathaniel's chips into a black drawstring bag and presented it to him on open palm.

Nathaniel dropped a red piece into the fae's hand as he took the bag.

The four of us turned toward the stairs.

Oleksandr's voice was low enough that only we could hear. "They're going to take us through the second deck. It's the only way to the stairs that lead up."

I nodded, but a chill nestled deep in my gut.

"Whatever you see there," Oleksandr said. "Don't stop. Don't react. It's a test."

A test to see how cool the humans would be. To see if we could earn our place up top. A numbness spread through me. What the hell was up there?

A pixie waved us up the stairs that clung to the outside of the boat. The steps stopped before a closed door. The entirety of the second deck was closed off, rolling doors clamped down. I could still hear the band playing from the first deck, but that only made the quiet before me more oppressive.

I took a deep breath as Oleksandr pushed the door open, dread coiling in my core.

Oleksandr stepped in first. I followed, blinking in the dim light. The wooden floorboards stretched before me, polished until they shone. The room was dotted here and there with displays. Petros' own personal museum.

A cage directly before us held a brightly colored parrot,

the red and green of its plumes glittered in the light. It perched on the limb of a twisted bare tree that stretched to the top of the cage. The bird cocked its head to the side, watching us.

"It's just a bird," I breathed, the dread easing in my gut.

"Hello," said the bird.

I jumped.

Nathaniel gave a low chuckle and passed me, walking further into the dim room.

Samuel threw me a sympathetic look.

It was just a parrot, I told myself, but I kept my eye on it as I skirted the cage. The bird didn't speak again.

I followed the other two across the floor, Oleksandr bringing up the rear.

Some of the cages were on stands, some sat on the floor. A few were covered in opaque lavender cloths. I wasn't sure if those were empty or whatever was inside was just sleeping. We walked amongst them with quiet steps, like treading through an empty church. But there was no hallowed ground here.

"Look," Nathaniel whispered. I hurried to catch up.

He had stopped before a cage little bigger than a cupboard. Inside I recognized the twitching nose, the long white ears, the small plump body.

"A kell."

"Kell aren't real," Samuel said, suddenly at our side.

"Sure they are," Nathaniel said. He ran a hand before the front of the cage, not close enough to touch, but near enough to attract the animal's attention. The kell hopped closer to the bars and sat back on its haunches, tracking Nathaniel's movements with its upper body.

"He's cute," I said, almost brave enough to step forward.

"Odd. He hasn't imprinted yet," Nathaniel said, dropping his hand.

"What do you mean imprinted?" Samuel asked.

The kell almost looked disappointed as the hand fell from view. It leaned forward, tiny paws pressing against the bars. Sharp canines flashed as it sniffed the air. I eyed the stand the cage rested on, hoping it was bolted in.

"Kell are bred to fight," Nathaniel explained. "In the wild, they're pack animals. Fiercely loyal to their den mothers. Poachers take them from their mothers before they have a chance to imprint on them. They transport them in harsh conditions, very careful not to show the animal any caring touch. They feed them with a mechanism, so the kell doesn't know who's giving them food. A precaution to keep it from imprinting on the smuggler before it can get to its owner."

The kell watched us with dark eyes. Tall ears twitched at Nathaniel's voice.

"Once it's sold," Nathaniel continued. "For an outrageous price, by the way. The new owner feeds it by hand and, tah-dah, you have a loyal fighter who would do anything to protect you." His voice lowered. "Even if that means you convince him that you're endangered by other kell, in a ring, with bright lights. For a decent amount of betting money, you've got yourself a prize fighter. Kells don't retire from that life. They die one way or another."

"That's terrible," I said. My heart swelled for the furry creature before us. I'd only ever known them to be dangerous. I'd never considered what might have made them that way. The dark eyes were locked on mine.

The kell looked soft, so very pettable.

"I still think it's just a bunny," Samuel said, breaking the spell the creature had on us.

"Shall we open the cage and find out?" Nathaniel asked.

Samuel opened his mouth to reply, but Oleksandr's voice cut in. "Come along, children."

He passed by us, a cold expectation that we should follow.

Samuel let out a grumble that sounded awfully close to *patronizing bastard*.

Nathaniel gave me a sympathetic smile as we turned away from the cage.

We were almost out the other side of the menagerie. Almost to the door that would lead upstairs when I felt a tug on my heart. I drew up short, letting the others get to the stairs before me.

It was as though a chain around my chest had drawn taught. I turned to my left, to the looming cage covered with lavender.

A corner of the cloth had folded back.

No, not a cage.

A tank.

My heart dropped. I tasted bile. I knew what had stopped me.

Before I could stop myself, I reached forward and pulled on the heavy drape. It billowed down like a sail falling from a top mast. My heart clenched tighter and tighter as it revealed more of the tank and finally the creature inside of it.

She lay at the bottom of the tank. Her eyes closed. Her skin was a deep brown, and coils of matted hair half obscured her face. Her dark obsidian tail, curled beneath her body. Flecks of gold glittered like stars between the scales.

I staggered forward a step and brought my hand up to the tank's surface.

Tatiana.

Her eyes snapped open, and she hurled herself against the glass. I jumped, tears stinging my eyes as she rammed her body against the tank wall over and over. She opened her mouth wide, and I prepared for the shriek of anger, but none came. Her mouth was empty, a stump left where her tongue should have been.

My hands flew to my own mouth before I even knew I was moving.

White scars stood out on the skin across her neck. They'd cut out her vocal cords. She couldn't sing.

She threw herself against the tank wall and water sloshed out of the grate at the top, running down the sides. A hissing sound escaped her lips, her face twisted in rage.

I raised a shaking hand toward her. *I'm getting you out,* I mouthed.

Before I could move, Oleksandr was back at my side. "What are you doing?" He demanded. "I told you not to touch anything."

"But she's—she's—"

How could I explain to him that I knew her? How could I tell him that without telling him what I was?

My heart ached as I let him push me up the stairs. I would come back for her, I told myself.

I'd get her out of that tank if it was the last thing I did on this godforsaken boat.

Nathaniel and Samuel met us at the top of the stairs. Samuel's eyes widened when he saw me. I can't imagine what he saw. My hands shook with rage or fear or adrenaline, it didn't matter. I clenched them into fists and then open again, pumping feeling back into them.

"Are you okay?" Samuel asked as I reached his side.

"I'm fine," I said. I rolled my shoulders back. Let's get this over with. I had another mission to get to when we were done and no clue how I was going to accomplish it.

We skirted around the gaming floor, near the low benches that rounded the top deck of *The Thorn*. Anyone not sitting at the gaming tables seemed to gravitate toward the benches to talk and drink and flirt. One was occupied by a shifter in hybrid form. He had to be some kind of a panther, rounded ears atop his furry head, dark spots barely visible in his dark fur. His arms wrapped around a petite blond; her face hidden by his massive head as they kissed.

Compared to the lower deck, this gaming floor was nearly silent. Music from the first deck band drifted up and the splash of water from the wheel, but other than that, only necessary words were spoken. Although I could swear I heard Tatiana's unvoiced screams from the deck below. I blinked once, clearing my gaze.

Silent waiters in their white uniforms drifted among the tables taking drink orders and delivering cocktails.

Oleksandr led us toward the foremost table. A group of three high fae sat around it, a blond male and female and a dark-haired male whose head was crowned with delicate twisted silver. My eyes narrowed at the sight of that crown. Petros. He was responsible for the menagerie downstairs.

All three faces were ethereal in their beauty, high cheek bones and angled eyes that flashed black and shining in the rising moon. Long pointed ears peeked out of silky hair that fell far down their backs. They should have been picturesque, but to me they looked vicious.

My gaze tunneled toward that foremost table, but I felt eyes on me as I walked up the deck. Shifter eyes that flashed gold in the moonlight, trailing down the silk material of my dress. Vampire eyes that glanced my way and dismissed me as less beautiful than they. Surely, this was what Oleksandr had in mind when he'd picked the sapphire gown. All eyes on the two of us, arm in arm as we paraded to the front of the boat. With Nathaniel and Samuel trailing behind, they looked like servants of ours, the perfect reason to have humans on a high fae riverboat.

There were two seats open at Petros' table, Oleksandr gestured Nathaniel into one, leaving Samuel standing behind his chair. Oleksandr took the other seat and pulled me onto his lap. I froze. His legs were cold beneath me, like sitting on a marble bench in the early morning before the sun rose. Showtime. I fixed a gentle smile on my face and leaned my side against his chest, draping my arms around his neck.

The dark-haired fae raised a glass of scarlet liquid our direction, a welcome to his table. I kept my smile gentle, resisting the urge to bare my teeth.

"Petros," Oleksandr said. He flashed a smile and dropped a cool hand onto my hip.

I glanced at Nathaniel. His face was neutral, steady. He looked like he belonged here.

Petros gestured for the game to continue.

A lesser fae dealt the cards. Aside from the three high fae and our two players, two other seats were occupied. One by an older man in an expensive looking black coat and tails. His eyes were a chilling green that matched the emerald broach at his throat. When he snapped for a waiter, green sparks flew from his fingertips.

In the last seat, black hair pulled to one side, revealing

the blue monarch on her neck, sat Hesta. She wore a halter top black dress, its neckline plunging deep below her sternum. And there, between the straps of fabric, was the Firestone. It hung low from a thick burgundy cord. A brilliant gem, amber glinting with an internal golden light.

Behind her, a massive thrall lurked. His shoulders were as broad as Harnock's, hands meaty like hammers. He stood still as a statue over her shoulder. Waiting for whatever order she might give.

She caught me staring and I gave her a lazy smile.

She flashed sharp fangs back at me and I increased my grin.

Oleksandr cocked his head back, his breath cool on my cheek. "You're making her nervous."

I let out a light laugh, hoping Hesta would be disarmed by our whispers and not driven from the table. "She's looking at us, isn't she? Not a single glance toward Samuel."

Oleksandr splayed his hand wide on my hip, stretching his fingers across my stomach. "Clever," he whispered. "I've always wanted to be a distraction."

I resisted the urge to throw his hands off me. He was teasing me. Pushing to see how far I'd let him go. Asshole.

A commotion from the direction we'd come raised our attention.

"Don't *touch me*, you absolute pig!"

The petite figure who had been with the were-panther stood now, pushing away from her companion. The panther's eyes flashed, teeth lengthening in his mouth. He snatched for her again. Claws tore into her dress as she twisted away, ripping the fabric into strips.

My thighs tensed. Oleksandr's hand tightened on my hip, warning me to stay still. I could blow our whole cover if I tried to intervene. But I couldn't just do nothing.

A blue ball of lightening rocketed over our heads. It felt almost cold as it passed me, like walking past an open freezer. It smashed into the were-panther, knocking him off the deck to splash into the river below. I looked to see who had cast it and there was Petros, his black eyes tinted blue, retaking his seat. He caught my stare and gave me a solemn nod.

I looked back to see a pair of waiters flank the young blond, guiding her toward the stairs and out of sight of the rest of the players.

I wondered where she went. Was she joining the menagerie? Did she see my kin in that tank and agree not to say anything when she left the boat? There was no way to follow now.

Our table was silent as the rest of the round played out. I eyed Petros across from me when I was sure he wasn't looking. The woman had been human. He'd stepped in to protect her when he didn't have to. Sure, it had protected the peace on his boat, but he could have just as easily moved the couple downstairs. He hadn't needed to intervene as he did. How could this be the same being who kept Tatiana down below?

"How about a change of game," Hesta asked as the round finished. "Hold 'em?"

The mage beside me growled. "Not a chance. Every time you get close to losing, you drop that infernal necklace into the pot and then no one can get their money."

Hesta's eyes gleamed. "Oh, you know that's not true. You love hold 'em."

The mage blinked once. His face losing all expression for a moment. "I love hold 'em," he repeated.

A chill crawled down my back. Her gift is forgetting.

With only her words. Hesta could use that on any of us. We had to act fast.

"I'm game," Oleksandr said, his voice rumbling in his chest against my side.

The high fae shrugged, but his two blond companions excused themselves. That left Nathaniel, Oleksandr, the mage, and Hesta. The dealer pulled a fresh deck from beneath the table and peeled open the packaging. Petros put a chip into the center of the table and each player followed suit.

A few shuffles and the cards were dealt. A seriousness took over the table as each player looked at their hand. Hesta bet first, matching the first set of chips.

I'd never been good at poker. Dad had tried to teach me to play once but laughed when I couldn't keep a straight face. I hadn't tried again.

Three cards flipped face up in the center of the table and more chips went into the center. No one folding yet. The mage beside us blew a breath out making his overgrown mustache dance. Was that a tell? I couldn't be sure.

The game was hard to follow when my thoughts kept drifting to the deck below.

One more card flipped into the center and the mage folded, everyone else holding strong. Oleksandr showed me his jack and seven. They were both hearts.

Nathaniel's face was still impassive as he tossed more chips into the pot. Oleksandr's eyes flashed as the fifth card was placed on the table. He and the high fae folded. It was just Hesta and Nathaniel, facing off across the table.

A predatory smile fixed on Hesta's face as she flipped her last chip forward. Nathaniel raised her bet by one and shot her a half smile. "You're out of funds."

Hesta tapped her cards on the table, thoughtfully. Once,

twice. She reached up and unhooked the necklace from her neck. With a thud that sounded louder than the single gem should make, she dropped it onto the pile of chips.

The mage beside us leaned forward, the gem reflecting in his eyes. "Gorgeous," he said.

Come on, Nathaniel. Win this one. It would be so much easier to win the necklace fair and square. Then I could get the others off the boat in peace and maybe we'd go back through the menagerie on the way out. I'd have a chance to do *something*.

Nathaniel pushed the rest of his chips into the center, a final bet.

Hesta flipped her two cards. "Full house," she crooned, pointing at the two fours in the river and additional jack. She reached for the pile of chips.

Nathaniel held up a hand and Hesta paused, face already forming into a grimace.

"Four of a kind," he said, turning his hand to reveal two more fours.

Everyone at the table held their breath. Hesta stared at the Firestone. "You can't take it," she said. "You can't pick it up."

Nathaniel held his neutral face and snapped his fingers once. Samuel leaned forward and plucked the necklace off the top of the stack.

The mage beside me gasped.

The high fae raised a dark eyebrow.

Nathaniel smiled.

Then, the thrall lunged.

Chips scattered across the deck as the table flipped. The thrall was on top of Samuel before I could even move. I threw myself at it, wrapping my legs around its torso and beating with my fists. Samuel thrust the Firestone into the thrall's chest, burning a hole straight through his ribs. I slipped off his back before the magic could touch me.

Hesta rose with a snarl and stalked through the empty space where the table had stood. She closed a hand around Nathaniel's throat and lifted him off the ground. "You should have folded, human."

Why wasn't the high fae intervening? He stood a few feet away from us, a quizzical expression on his face as he stared at Samuel.

Oleksandr stepped up to Hesta's side and tapped her on the shoulder. "Clan Montrose, is it?" he asked. "Does Lady Grendel know how it is you are spending your evenings?"

Hesta turned to face him, hurling Nathaniel away from her. "You wouldn't dare tell her," she said.

I scrambled to Nathaniel's side, gown trailing on the deck behind me.

"I don't believe we've met," Oleksandr said, his smile as bright as I'd ever seen it. "My name is Oleksandr." His voice dropped to a growl. "Oleksandr Keiran."

Hesta yelped and stepped back a pace as though she had been burned.

"I don't think your matriarch would take kindly to you cheating at cards instead of minding your clan's business," Oleksandr pressed. "Maybe I should give her a call now."

"No," Hesta said. "Don't. I wasn't cheating. I was—I was—"

"And losing a Firestone," Oleksandr tsked. "My, my. What a disgrace you're about to be."

Samuel was beside me, helping Nathaniel to his feet. The Firestone hung around my partner's neck, dangling from its burgundy cord once more.

Petros moved. He seemed to have been waiting until the

scuffle was over, but now he pointed one finger in Samuel's direction. "Bring him to me."

White uniforms came from all directions. They had been gathering, circling us, waiting for their leader's command while we squabbled over the Firestone and revealed to everyone watching that Samuel couldn't be harmed by it.

"Over the side," I yelled. "Now!"

Samuel ducked under a pair of arms that tried to tackle him and sprang onto the railing of the boat. I started to move but my dress tightened around my middle, and I crashed to the ground. A pixie had grabbed ahold of my train. He pulled the sapphire fabric toward himself winding it up, dragging me across the deck.

"Go," I called to Samuel. He looked torn for a second, looking between me and the water below.

Nathaniel got to his feet and tackled Samuel; they both went over the edge.

I turned toward the pixie who held my gown and landed a kick square in his gut. A grunt of pain and my dress was free. I flew across the deck, barely registering the white-clad figures who grabbed at me. The dress tore at my shoulder, the train ripping behind me as a desperate grasp was made.

I surprised my pursuers by veering away from the boat's railing. It only took them a half second to recover, but that was all I needed. I ran toward the stern of the ship, toward the stairs that led down. A plan was just beginning to take shape in my mind. I pulled a plate of hors d'oeuvres from the side of a craps table, dodging around gaping patrons.

The chill of a blue lightning ball bathed my left arm with ice as it flew past me. I shifted right and kept running. I reached the stairs and threw myself down them, feet barely touching the steps as I careened toward the door at the bottom. A twist of the knob and I was in, slamming the door and leaning against it panting.

The door shuddered as someone slammed into it from the other side. I prayed the deadlock would hold.

Tatiana glared at me from her tank, her tail whipping like a black snake, agitating the waters.

"I told you I'd come back for you," I said.

No recognition lit up her eyes. She twisted her mouth in a hiss. Did she even remember me? Did she even know who I was?

Another blow against the door and then the sound of quick steps back up the stairs. My pursuers had to be going to get something they could use to ram it open. We didn't have much time.

I jumped toward the tank, curling my fingers over the lip of it and hoisting myself up. Water splashed against my shins as I knelt on the grate. Tatiana curled beneath me, shrinking down to the bottom of the tank.

"I'm not going to hurt you." I ran my fingers around the edges of the grate, searching for a clasp or a lock or something I could pry open. There was none. The metal seemed to be welded into the frame of the tank.

"How am I going to get you out of here?" I murmured half to myself.

Tatiana surged from the water, wrapping her hands around the grate, and tugging down. I yelped as the metal bowed beneath me. Brown eyes stared at me under the water, urgency in their gaze. She'd been working on the grate. Of course. I would have done the same every second of my captivity. She only needed a little help.

I stood atop the tank, hoping she could see in my eyes what I was trying to convey. I raised three fingers to her, dropped one, another, and then the last and jumped. Just as I landed, she pulled down on the metal. The grate let out a loud creak but didn't dislodge. I stood again, raised three fingers.

The door beside the tank exploded open.

I threw myself to the floor, rolling as I landed. Four lesser fae, green skin appearing sickly in the dim light, barged into the room. Two of them held pistols with flashlights attached to the muzzle. They advanced into the room. The other two lingered near the door, silver knives clenched tightly in each hand.

I backed through the room, keeping low to the floor. I didn't fancy being shot during a rescue mission. If I could get them separated, I could take them down one at a time.

Tatiana let out a hiss as one flashlight illuminated her tank, she sank back down to the bottom, making herself as small as possible.

An empty cage before me, covered with lavender cloth kept me from view. I held my breath as I listened for the fae's footsteps. They were so damn quiet.

The plate of hors d'oeuvres had flown across the floor when I entered the room. Now, the plate gleamed at my feet. I snatched it up. A thin ceramic of some kind, painted white. Hello, new distraction.

I hurled the plate across the room to shatter against the far wall. All four fae pivoted that direction. I took the opportunity to scuttle closer to the next phase of my rapidly forming plan. The cage near the middle of the deck. White ears twitched above my head as I crouched beside it.

Nathaniel had better be right about the kell's story. I reached a hand up and unlatched the cage. The kell landed on the deck before me on soft paws. I held my breath as he stretched his paws up toward my chest. His whiskers tickled my cheek as he scented my breath.

The four fae were calling to each other in a language I didn't understand. They must have found the shards of plate and realized what had happened.

I opened my hand, a small square of puff pastry stuffed with salmon and cream cheese sat on my palm. The kell dropped down to its haunches and took my hand between its two paws. A flashlight beam passed over us and I shrank instinctively.

The kell watched me with small inquisitive eyes, leaned forward, and took the pastry. Its nose twitched as it chewed. Suddenly, it was on my shoulder, nuzzling against my neck. I brought my hands up to its silky fur and whispered, "Protect me."

The kell dropped to the floor and disappeared, hopping away impossibly fast.

I followed the sounds of the first screams, crawling across the floor as the second flashlight beam swung wildly above me. The pool of blood was spreading across the floor, spurting from a bite taken out of the lesser fae's neck. I pulled the pistol from the dying fae's grasp, dropping the magazine into my hand to count the rounds left before sliding it back into the gun. I had three rounds. Three rounds for three fae. Assuming there were no more coming.

Another scream sounded across the deck and the two fae by the door began shouting. Make that three rounds for two fae.

I moved faster now, knowing the last firearm had been accounted for. A flash of metal in the lights above had me throwing myself to the floor as a knife arched through the air where I had just been. Shit. Of course, they could throw them. Rookie move.

I crawled between the legs of an exhibit stand and took aim at the fae by the door. The one on the left had his head turned, yelling up the stairs for help. I closed my right eye and trained my sights on him. Breathe in, out, squeeze the trigger.

The bullet buried itself in the doorframe beside him. Dammit. I was still shooting too far right. Down to two rounds.

A blur of white attached itself to the neck of the other fae, he hit the ground with a strangled cry. Hell yeah. Say hello to my very little, furry friend.

The fae I had in my sights, turned and fled up the stairs. In a moment, a small white and red ball bounced after him.

We didn't have long before Petros sent reinforcements down. I was shocked they hadn't arrived yet. No time to keep working on the grate above the tank. I took aim from across the room, guiding my muzzle slightly to the left of the tank.

"Stay down," I yelled. A half second later, I pulled the trigger.

A crack sounded across the room. The tank spider-webbed with broken glass, but the second layer held. I hoped shards weren't cutting into Tatiana's skin. I blew out another breath, kept my aim to the tank's left, and tightened around the trigger again.

The tank exploded out in a rush of water, I hurried across the deck, careful not to slip in the torrent. I dropped to Tatiana's side and grasped under her arms, half dragging her across the deck. My mind was on one track. Get to the door and off the side.

Tatiana hissed as her tail scraped along the glass that glittered on the wooden floorboards. Shit. Why wasn't she transforming? Her eyes darted around the room, wide with fear. She was moving on instinct alone.

"Let's go," I urged, pulling her along. Her tail whipped behind us, pushing her forward slower than I'd like.

Pounding footsteps on the stairs had me stepping behind her shoving her forward. A trail of blood led along the floor at my feet. Tatiana was bleeding more than I had first thought. I had to get her to the water, it would heal her. I turned toward the open door, standing between it and the injured melusine behind me.

The first two lesser fae could just be seen stepping onto the bottom step.

"*Stop*," I called out. Raising my voice, not in a potesta's command, but in a siren song.

"*Stay where you are.*"

The two froze. Tatiana twisted behind me, a gasp escaping her lips, past her mangled tongue. That voice, she recognized.

I scooped her up, straining to lift the weight of her tail. She transformed in my arms, shrinking down to what she really was, a small, scared girl. She tangled her hands in the cloth of my dress. Holding onto me. I pressed my back against the door and pushed us out to the walkway around the second deck. With a heave, I dropped Tatiana over the side to the river below.

I got one last look at a horde of white-clad fae and pixies pushing around the two who were frozen stiff on the stairs before the door closed between us, and I vaulted over the railing.

Chapter Twenty-Three

I transformed as I hit the water, kicking off my shoes and tearing away the remnants of the skirt that dragged me deeper. My tail unfurled like a sail, swishing through the water with powerful strokes. I tore at the bodice of the dress, finger's scrabbling at the zipper as my gills tried to open underneath. Finally, I wriggled out of it and pulled in river water, blowing out the air that had been trapped in my lungs.

The dark shape of Tatiana swam far away from me, black tail pushing her through the water far faster than I expected. She was moving toward the Gulf. I let her go. It would only be selfish for me to chase after her, demand that she listen to my apologies for how we'd left things. She'd be fine now that she was free in the water.

The cool river ran over my skin and scales. It calmed me like a hug, like a warm familiar blanket. I reached out with my senses, searching for Nathaniel and Sammy. Their presence far behind me. A surge of my tail and I was barreling toward them. The water caressing my cheeks.

I surfaced right beside them, and they both yelped.

"You okay?"

Nathaniel nodded, wiping water from his eyes.

"Yeah," Samuel said. The Firestone lit up the water around him, bright with its internal glow. "What happened to you?"

"I got held up. You didn't have to wait for me." I looked around the surface of the water, undisturbed save for the slight current below. "Let's head to shore, we've got to get back to the Agency before that high fae can turn the boat around for us." I nodded at Samuel. "He was awfully interested in you."

Samuel kicked toward the shore, stripping off his coat as he went.

I turned to Nathaniel, about to push him along, but the river beside me was empty.

What the hell?

He splashed to the surface, water spraying. "Meranda," he gasped. His eyes wide with terror. "I can't—"

He went under again. Was pulled under. And suddenly, I felt them.

I dove.

Ghostly sailors grasped Nathaniel's arms, dragging him down to the river floor. The river was almost two hundred feet deep here. He couldn't hold his breath all that way. They were going to kill him. Drown him as they believed he should have drowned years ago.

I let out a piercing scream, sending my power through the water. I couldn't control the ghosts as a potesta, but the water was my domain, and they were trespassing in it.

My tail beat a current against them, buffeting them away from their captain. His eyes were already rolling back. I was sure his lungs burned for air. The surface was too far above us. I wrapped my arms around him and pressed my lips to his own, offering my breath to him.

His eyes widened and he pushed me away, but I gripped him tighter. *Breathe, idiot.*

With one arm around his waist, I pushed off the riverbed and swam up. He was light in the water and my tail was strong, but still his coat held us back. I stripped it off him as we went.

We hit the surface and he gasped in a breath. I held him up as he coughed, water and snot pouring from him.

Samuel stood on the shore. "Are you okay?"

I pushed Nathaniel toward him, and Samuel grasped under his arms, pulling him out.

Ghostly hands clawed down my tail, and I let out a yelp. The sailors from the water climbed over me, stabbing and clawing as they went. I beat them back, but without iron, my fists passed right through them. The salty smell of my own blood met my nostrils, staining the water around me dark.

More sailors were on the shore, surrounding Nathaniel and Samuel where they stood shivering.

"You're their captain," I called. "Command them."

Nathaniel gave me a look of distress. "I'm not their captain."

"Command them," I yelled before ghostly hands dragged me back into the water.

I couldn't drown. That wasn't a danger for me in the river, but the hands that grabbed at me were chilled and sharp. They passed through me, leaving freezing cold behind. A ghost sickness setting into my bones. A hand on my chest and it felt as though my heart would stop.

Then a call surged through the water, reverberating off, river rock and silt.

Stop.

I broke through the surface, throwing myself onto the shore and shaking with cold.

Samuel placed a hand on me, his palm hot against my skin.

We watched as Tanner approached Nathaniel. The rest of the sailors holding back.

"You abandoned us," Tanner hissed. "You were supposed to be there for us."

"You mutinied," Nathaniel spat. "What was I supposed to do, stay in the hold as the ship went down."

"Yes," Tanner howled. "You've cursed us!"

"You cursed yourself," Nathaniel said.

Tanner wanted to lunge at him, I could see it in his face, but invisible hands held him back. The power of Nathaniel's command stayed him.

"You must set us free," Tanner said. "You must die so you can guide us on."

Nathaniel cast a look my direction, imploring.

"They believe you are the true captain," I said. "The ones who followed Tanner were able to pass on when he died. These sailors believed in you. And Tanner is stuck here because he knew the truth."

"You led us in life," one sailor called out. "You were a good captain."

Nathaniel shook his head, his jaw clenching. "I wasn't a good captain," he said. "You deserved better. You deserved a captain who wouldn't lead you head on into a storm in order to make a deadline. You deserved a captain who could see beyond his own greed to the way you all were suffering. Tanner was right to take command."

The sailors flickered once. My chest ached.

Nathaniel's eyes were bright in the moonlight. "I was

proud and selfish," he said. "I'm sorry I wasn't the captain you needed. You would all be alive today if it weren't for me." His voice broke on the last word.

Tanner shuddered. His shoulders sagged.

A tear dropped to Nathaniel's cheek, glittering like a diamond. "Can you forgive me?" he whispered.

The sailors around the shoreline looked at one another, questions in their eyes.

"Tanner should have been your captain," he said. "He worked to guide us out of the storm. He wasn't blind to your suffering."

Sailors flickered again, their hold on this world waning as their loyalties shifted. Their true captain already dead with them. I wondered if they could see the light.

Nathaniel placed a hand on Tanner's shoulder. He didn't even flinch from the chill. "Tanner, the *Sea Wraith* is yours. You are her true captain."

Tanner closed his eyes, a ghostly breath escaping his lips. A light bloomed in each sailor's chest, growing and growing until it consumed them. I closed my eyes against the brightness. When I opened them again, the sailors were gone.

Nathaniel alone crouched on the shoreline, hands covering his eyes as his shoulders shook.

Brigitte was thrilled that we'd made it back with no visible injuries. I didn't tell her all that had happened, but I watched Nathaniel warily as he took a seat on Dad's couch and stared at the floor. His clothes were still damp from the river. He only moved to change when I pulled him up by the arm and walked him to the bathroom.

I brewed a pot of tea and brought it into Dad's office on a tray laden with cups and a bowl of sugar cubes. Samuel fiddled with the Firestone still hanging around his neck.

"How are we going to get this to Poincare?" he asked. "We can't exactly hand it to him."

"I'll call ahead and let him know it's been keyed to someone else," I said. "He must have a mage or something he can call on to fix that."

Samuel shrugged and let the stone hang free. I guess Sammy had to come to the drop off with me tomorrow.

I handed him a teacup. He'd changed into a maroon sweater and dark jeans. Holding the tea, he looked positively cozy.

Nathaniel settled onto the couch again, back in his white t-shirt and blue jeans. I was in the habit of leaving an old blue blanket on the back of the couch. Nathaniel didn't move when I placed it over his shoulders. I didn't know how long it would take him to snap out of whatever state he was in, but I could at least keep him warm until he found his way out of it.

Brigitte ordered a few pizzas and Samuel demanded one with pineapple on it. They bickered for a few moments before a compromise was reached. I sat behind Dad's desk and turned on his computer. I recycled the wi-fi, hardly any optimism left that it would work. The screen refreshed.

I blinked.

"Internet's up," I said.

"What?" Samuel crossed the room.

"Oleksandr was tinkering with your router this afternoon," Nathaniel said, looking up from the floor. "He said you were taking too long getting ready and the collection of wires and plugs was a fire hazard."

A small light was back in Nathaniel's eyes when he looked at me. I prayed it wouldn't dim back down.

"Thank the universe for vampires with a penchant toward technology," I murmured.

A scratching sounded from the front door and Samuel and Brigitte went to bring in the pizzas.

I watched Nathaniel pick at a loose thread on the couch arm. The lines in his face were deep. The frown more pronounced.

We'd come back uninjured, but we weren't whole.

Not all of us.

I wasn't sure even the pizza could fix that. Pineapple or not.

A yell sounded from the door, and I started around the desk, certain that someone was breaking in. A white ball of fur tore across the office floor and slammed into my legs. The kell sat at my feet, raising its front paws to rest on my knees, stretching towards me.

Nathaniel looked from me to the kell, his eyebrows rising by the second.

I reached down and picked it up. The kell snuggled into my arms, burying its whiskered nose into my chest.

"Well, hello there," I said, running my fingers between its ears. The last I'd seen it, the furball was covered in blood, looking for its next victim. No blood stood out on its white fur now, but its paws were mud-stained. I couldn't imagine it jumped off the boat into the Mississippi after us, but how else had it found me?

Samuel came around the corner. "Is that what I think it is?"

"Sammy," I said. "I think you owe my kell an apology for not believing in its existence."

A rumbling sound started deep in its chest. It vibrated

in my arms like a steering wheel on a bumpy road. They purred?

Samuel held up a hand. "No," he said. "There's no way that's real."

My nose was already beginning to run. Damn, I needed a tissue.

Brigitte peeked over his shoulder. "Of course it's real," she said. "And it's cute. Hello, little—what are you naming him?"

My mind blanked. Three sets of eyes stared at me expectantly. I couldn't think of a single name. The purr stopped. The kell leaned its head back until its black eyes were fixed on me too.

"Uhm—" A word popped into my head. I said it without vetting first. "Fluff Nugget."

Brigitte groaned.

"I don't know," I said. "I didn't expect to run into this problem tonight. My brain thought it was done working for the day."

A knock sounded on the Agency door. Samuel left to answer it. I hoped it really was the pizza this time, any distraction from the animal in my arms. Which had, apparently, fallen asleep. Fluff Nugget turned so I could see the tiny heart-shaped pads under his paws.

"You're impossible," Brigitte said.

"Valentine," Nathaniel said, his blue eyes found mine. "He only has eyes for you."

I smiled down at the tiny ball of fur. "Valentine."

The kell's nose twitched. I leaned down and kissed his soft forehead. The smell of dirty water and blood hit my senses. Valentine needed a bath.

Epilogue

"Okay, but you can't stay too late," Brigitte called as I raced past her. "Homecoming is tomorrow."

"We won't be late," I called, dropping the grocery bags onto her kitchen counter. "It's one movie."

Valentine draped himself over my shoulder, his paws reaching down to bat at the plastic bag.

"What did you bring?" Brigitte closed the front door behind Nathaniel and caught the disc case he tossed to her. "The Notebook?"

"Meranda said it was one of your favorites," Samuel called from beside me. He pulled a package of cherry licorice bits out of the grocery bag and dumped them into a bowl.

The check from Poincare had cleared that afternoon. The Agency was safe for the time being, and it had taken very little convincing to drag Samuel to the grocery store for movies and junk food.

"I voted for Mad Max, but they overruled me," I said.

Brigitte smiled.

Nathaniel helped her set up the television, while Samuel and I popped some popcorn. The smell of butter filled the small living room as the four of us crowded onto the couch. Brigitte and I sat in between the other two. Valentine stretched out on the couch back behind me.

"I really need to get another chair in here," Brigitte said as Samuel took a handful of popcorn out of the bowl in her lap.

The title sequence started, music blaring from the speakers and sending Samuel scrabbling for the remote.

"I like it," I whispered back. "It's cozy."

I eyed Nathaniel where he sat beside me, his hip pressed against mine. He had one elbow on the couch arm, the side of his head in his palm. I could tell from the glazed look in his eyes, he wasn't actually seeing the images on the screen.

He'd been that way since sending his crew away. It had taken everything out of him. I'd let him stay on the couch in Dad's office that first night. Content to watch him across the room while I guided the computer through updates.

He hadn't tried to leave, and I hadn't asked him to. As far as I was concerned, the Agency could use someone with his expertise. We'd have to find a different sleeping arrangement than an office couch, though.

I held out a bowl of sour gummy worms and he startled as it entered his vision.

I gave him a smile and he took one, examining it for a moment before biting off a piece.

It would be a long road, I knew. But we'd be fine.

We had to be.

Poincare had put the word out that our Agency had

serviced his needs. Phone calls were already rolling in. Collier Investigative Agency was back in business.

But not tonight. Tonight was movie night.

A sniffle sounded beside me.

I passed Brigitte the tissues.

Acknowledgments

There are so many people I'd like to thank for helping to make this book all it could be.

Firstly, Eloise, my amazing critique partner, thank you for being my cheerleader, my late night hype woman, my friend.

My editor, Katie. I owe you a taco.

Kevin J. Anderson for continuing to pour your insights and knowledge out so generously.

Mark Leslie Lefebvre for continuing to encourage me.

My family for putting up with everything, even during a move, and a new job, and night shift.

Especially Dad. I love you.

My readers, it's all for you.

Love to you all.

Soli Deo Gloria

About the Author

jjlynndaniels.com

From Southern California to Middle Tennessee, by way of the Rocky Mountains, JJ Lynn Daniels has maintained her love for writing and publishing across the United States.

When not writing books, raising her three daughters, teaching her German Shepherd mix new tricks, or working nightshift in an emergency room, JJ likes to sit on the back porch with a hot cup of coffee and a good book.

JJ will complete her Master's in Publishing in August 2023.

JJ Lynn Daniels is the author of The Metal's Bane Series and The Meranda Haley Series.

About the Publisher

B. Shepherd Publications LLC was formed in 2022 by founder JJ Lynn Daniels. The imprint specializes in stories that build resiliency and antifragility in their readers.

May resistance make you stronger.

B. Shepherd Publication's flagship author is JJ Lynn Daniels.

bshepherdpublications.com